Table of Contents

Mercy's Gift

CYNDI RAYE

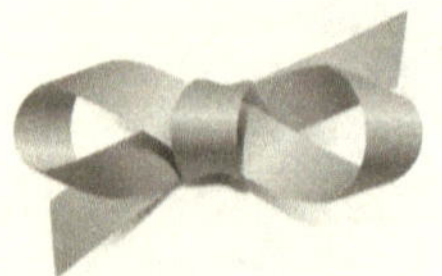

Mercy's Gift
The Belles of Wyoming
Book 8
by
Cyndi Raye
Virginia McKevitt (Illustrator)

The Belles are at it again. Join the town of Belle, Wyoming in another 5 book series with an Easter Holiday theme. There are 5 books in this series from book #6 to #10.

---

1. http://www.CyndiRaye.com

Chapter 1

Franklyn Mason hesitated at the door to the sheriff's office, his hands deep in his pockets. He had to get this over and done with before he was able to move on with his life. Taking a solid deep breath, he pushed open the door to the sound of bells jingling overhead. "Congrats on the job, Sheriff."

David Knight looked up. His eyes widened at first then he quickly stood. "Frank! Welcome back to Belle! It's been, what, four years?"

He reached out for David's hand and shook it. Everyone in town called him Frank, even though at medical school he was known as Franklyn. It didn't matter, he was home and he no longer had to be called by that name. It was good to see a childhood friend. "I reckon it's been about that long. Got my medical degree now so I can put doctor in front of my name."

"Congratulations. I know you worked hard. Come in and take a load off."

The sheriff pulled out the wooden chair beside his desk for Frank to sit down on. He was a might uncomfortable knowing the conversation that had to take place. So he dived in immediately, figuring to get it over with first thing. "I came to you right off the stage. I have to get everything squared away first before I can hold my head up in public."

The sheriff raised a brow. "You trying to redeem yourself, Frank?"

Frank grinned. "I believe I am."

"Well, thanks for coming to me, but you don't have an issue with me. I'll admit I was angry at you at first and wanted to ring your neck until things turned around for Hope and I. My wife, on the other hand, does have an issue with you. One that I am hoping you can clear up."

He nodded, ashamed of his behavior. "I can't explain what happened when I was in Philadelphia, but I knew deep in my heart Hope and I were not meant to be married."

David slapped Frank on the back. "Thank the good Lord for that! I'm afraid the complications you caused had me sending for a mail order bride."

"You are joking, right?"

David shook his head. "I'm afraid not. When I came home after years away, I found out Hope was engaged to you. I didn't think I ever had a chance with her and someone talked me into ordering a mail order bride. Thank my lucky stars her father became ill and she never showed up."

A wide smile crossed Frank's face. He was so relieved. "I knew you and Hope were best friends growing up, but husband and wife? David, I'm happy for you."

"Thanks for not going through with the wedding. Although, you do owe her an explanation. Come by the house tonight for supper. We'll talk then."

Frank left David's office feeling much lighter in spirit. He had thought he'd get punched in the face when he walked in, or arrested. Even though he didn't break the law, some people had their way of getting back at others. He was a lucky man that David was not that type of person.

Frank picked up his suitcase and headed towards his old home. He took a right off of Main street to Tall Pine Lane. A few feet around the corner stood a rather large Victorian home with its shutters closed and the porch bare. Tall pines lined the street and the backdrop. He stared for a few minutes, wishing his mother's sweet face would show up at the window like it had for so many years. He knew it would never happen again for she was on the hill looking out over Belle, Wyoming.

His loving mother had wanted to be buried alongside her husband. Frank had no one to come home to now. They'd never call him doctor. Both his parents were gone, he wasn't even sure why he was home. It would've been so easy to keep going, to accept a position at the Philadelphia Hospital after he passed his exam.

Yet, he had some unfinished business in Belle to take care of. Not only did he need to explain to Hope why he hadn't been able to marry her at the time, but he had come home for another reason.

His eyes wandered to the house next door. It was almost identical to his parents house except the windows weren't boarded shut. It even had the same front porch. There were flowers in baskets and pots on the front steps leading to the front door, along with a few chairs. The house looked lived in so he knew she was still there.

The woman he had always loved.

The reason he didn't keep his promise to Hope's mother.

Mercy.

<> <> <>

She peeked out the upstairs window, careful to hide her radiant red hair behind the curtain. Her heart beat twice as hard seeing him for the first time in four years. He was taller and his physique was built up more. She put her hand to her heart, afraid he'd hear it pumping from behind the window.

Frank was the man she had adored all these years. Not many knew that fact. The only one who did was his mother and she was long gone. She had invited Mercy to dinner many times, but mostly Frank had ignored her since she was the next door neighbor kid.

Her parent's had forbade her to look at any boys and even though Frank was allowed to come over on occasion, her mother watched him like a hawk. He always stayed for dessert and left right afterwards, telling them he needed to study. He was going to be a doctor someday.

Her parents had been friends with Frank and Hope's parents since they all lived on Tall Pines Lane. The adults would spend Sunday afternoons together going out for walks sometimes, leaving the three kids together. She never thought Hope had any interest in Frank and he never seemed to take his nose out of a book long enough to notice either one of them.

After Hope's mother and father passed away, he told everyone he promised her mother he'd take care of Hope now that she had no one. The next thing Mercy knew, Frank was engaged to Hope. Anger and resentment for Hope had caused a rift in their friendship for a few years. She was lucky if they spoke more than once a year. It was a shame, she missed her old friend.

She watched as Frank set his carpetbag on the ground next to him and stared at his house. Several times he looked over to hers. She slid further back to make sure her hair didn't give her away. After several minutes, he picked up his bag and walked to his own house that had sat empty since his parents passed away.

When he disappeared inside, Mercy let out her breath and moved away from the curtain. If she poked her head out the window, all he had to do was look out a window to find her watching him.

Perhaps it was time to welcome him home. They were older now. She'd be able to see him face to face without yearning for him, wouldn't she?

Besides, it would be unkind of her to ignore him. Neighbors always welcomed anyone who came to Belle, especially someone who had come back home like he had. She checked herself in the mirror. Satisfied, she picked up the white crème cake she had baked earlier this morning and walked out the door, almost stumbling when she stood face to face with Frank!

"Oh!" She stepped back, the cake in her hands about to topple over. He caught it in one swoop and gave her a smile so wide she almost toppled in those arms, too.

Which, she noticed right away, were much larger than she had remembered. He was taller now, and his beautiful dark eyes watched her with amusement. Unlike years ago, they were no longer stuffed in a book.

Mercy had always been a bit unsteady on her feet, but to almost fall in his arms was a bit embarrassing.

"Steady now," he told her, his light touch on her shoulder setting off warning signals in her brain.

She took another step back, moving away. "Well," she laughed lightly, "the cake is for you. I wanted to welcome you home."

He nodded, tilting his head to stare at her. "Thank you, Mercy. It's been a long time. I'm happy to see you."

Was he? Or, was he being polite since she almost fell coming out of her own front door. She decided to keep the conversation cordial. "Hello, Franklyn. What brings you here to my house?"

He grinned. "You've always called me Frank, so does everyone else here."

"I know, which is why I didn't understand why our wonderful town gossip told us your new name is Doctor Franklyn Mason. So, I will call you Dr. Mason."

"Suit yourself, but I always liked the way you said Frank."

He had? This was something she didn't know. Maybe he was paying attention when she thought he wasn't. Interesting. Yet, she had to ignore his casual indifference. "Those days are long gone, Dr. Mason. You are now an important addition to society with a doctor's degree and as far as I'm concerned, you must be treated in such a way not to offend you. The cake is for you."

He took a step closer.

Her eyes widened.

She backed up but the door hit her back and she stopped suddenly.

"Please call me Frank. I want to thank you for the cake."

"Your welcome," she said.

"No, I really appreciate this," he told her, looking at the cake and then her.

"It's nothing, really. I'm sure you will receive many more gifts like it until everyone welcomes you home."

He took another step closer. She felt the warmth from his body radiate between them. Oh, dear! Was he going to kiss her? Impossible! They had been neighbors and acquaintances growing up.

She was not expecting a kiss.

She looked up at him, her eyes wide and her curiosity now peaked.

He leaned down, touching her cheek with his mouth. "Thank you," he said softly, his low voice for her ears only.

When he turned around to leave, she wasn't sure why he was there in the first place. She called out. "What did you want?"

He turned, giving her a knowing look. "To see you."

She shook her head. "No," she whispered, although he had turned his back and was heading across the yard.

She went back inside and closed the door, feeling breathless. Leaning against it, she touched her hand to her cheek. Four long years she had waited to tell Franklyn Mason that he had hurt her. Then, the first thing he does is stare at her with those dark eyes and kiss her cheek.

How was she supposed to react when he didn't even know she liked him! It was her own fault he didn't know. She gazed at her image in the mirror that was hung on the wall right inside the front door.

Her eyes were wide, her nose red and her cheeks even redder. Mercy closed her eyes for a moment, dreaming that he had come home for her.

Then she stood up, pulled her shoulders back and put such a thought out of her mind. He probably came home to sell the house he grew up in. She had heard some of the gossip mongers in town talk about his dream of becoming one of those doctors in a big city like Philadelphia or even New York City.

She was certain he wasn't staying. There was no reason for her to even think he may be interested in her. His actions were friendly, weren't they? No reason to believe anything else.

She nodded at the image in the mirror. *This is just a stop along the way for him to tie up loose ends. Do not let your emotions get the best of you! No matter what!*

Mercy tried to get on with her day, baking another cake to take to the school function that evening. Even as she tried to deliberately close her mind to the sweet kiss on the cheek, she kept playing those five minutes over and over in her mind.

Would she ever get over Frank? Missing him the past four years had been tough, but she always had hope he'd come home someday and take notice of her.

His words right before he kissed her cheek reminded her that he was here. It wasn't a dream or a hopeful wish.

What did you want, she had asked him.

To see you, he had told her.

She wasn't quite sure what he meant.

Chapter 2

• • ❧ • •

FRANK WALKED BY MERCY'S house on his way to supper. It didn't appear as if she were at home, but she did have her own life. What did he think, she was there waiting for him to come visit?

The thought of Mercy on a date bothered him more than he realized. He hadn't thought much about her courting someone else these past four years, until he saw her again. What if she was in love with another man? He'd have to show her somehow that he cared. How was he going to do that when they had been solely neighbors and friends all these years? He knew his nose had been stuck in books while they were all growing up. Which reminded him, he'd have to swing by the library to see if they wanted some of his old books he had lying around the place.

For now, he had to face Hope. It wouldn't be easy. The way he had treated her was not right. He had stayed so busy in medical college there hadn't been much time to write back to her. Although she had never failed to send him a letter once a month. He had meant to write back, except his heart hadn't been in it and he had kept putting it off. Maybe he had been trying to tell her that without telling her.

Still, it did not excuse him from what he had done. He stood in front of the sheriff's door, ready to lift a hand to knock when the hairs on the back of his neck rose up. Someone's eyes were on him. He turned to find Mercy walking down the street holding another cake in her hand. She quickly avoided his gaze until he shouted out. "Mercy! Where are you going?"

She stumbled and he thought for a moment he'd have to rescue her again, but she found her footing and turned to him. "To the school. There's a dessert social tonight and I volunteered to help."

"Well, what better timing. I'm sure I'll be able to stop in after having dinner with the Sheriff and his wife."

Mercy nodded and kept on walking, as if she were talking to a casual neighbor. Which, he was or had been most of their life. Except he'd always had a crush on her and now she was treating him the same as anyone else. When he kissed her cheek earlier, maybe he went too far, but he thought she seemed pleased.

"Well, good evening, Doctor Mason!" Holly's sweet voice had him turning completely around..

"Hello, Holly, or should I say Mrs. Knight?"

She gave him a hug and invited him in. "Holly is fine. Please, do come in." He was surprised she was being so pleasant after everything he had put her through. This was going to be difficult to get through if she was this nice. He deserved to be yelled at, or reprimanded.

Placing his jacket on the coat hook, he followed the sheriff and his wife to the table, where they all sat down and prayed. When the food was served, not one word was mentioned about his behavior.

He wanted to get it out of the way. "Holly, I came here tonight to apologize to you."

She looked at her husband first with so much adoration it took Frank back. She truly was in love with her husband. Perhaps so much that what he had done no longer mattered. It probably mattered more to Frank. Still, he needed to apologize.

"Frank, I think I understand why you never wrote."

He was surprised. "You do."

"Yes. I am afraid I just witnessed the reason why and she was walking past our house when I answered the door."

His eyes flashed and he stared at her in shock. Was he that obvious? He was about to explain when she put up a hand.

The sheriff spoke up. "I think she has forgiven you, Frank."

"Yes, I have. I now realize you have loved Mercy all this time. Am I right?" Her soft voice went through him. He wanted to deny it.

"I'm sorry, Holly. I'm sorry about the way I treated you, not answering your letters. If I'd have written sooner, you'd have saved a lot of trouble."

She reached across the table and patted his hand. "If you'd have written, my husband and I may have never gotten together. Please, it's over and done with and I accept your apology."

"Thank you."

"That still doesn't answer the main question here, does it?" She was persistent if anything.

He looked at her husband. David shrugged and gave him one of those looks that said you had better answer her question or she won't stop until you do.

Frank sighed. "I didn't realize I loved Mercy until I left Belle and went to Philadelphia. She was all I thought about even when I got your letters. I'm sorry, Holly."

Holly smiled. "No need to be, Frank. You helped me during a horrendous time of my life and I will be forever grateful to you. I'm afraid my friendship with Mercy faltered during that time and hasn't been the same since. Now, I know why."

He was confused. "What do you mean?"

Holly stared at him as if he should know the answer. "Mercy is in love with you, too. She loved you even before you left for medical school. Sitting here piecing it all together makes perfect sense. The two of you have loved each other and never told each other!"

Frank was shocked. "Mercy? She loves me? Did she tell you that?"

Holly rolled her eyes. "She doesn't have to, I figured it all out. I'm afraid I owe her an apology, too."

"Now, sweetheart, don't go interfering in other peoples business. Maybe you should let dead dog's lie." The sheriff was always so matter of fact. Frank was glad he hadn't changed. At least there was something that had remained the same.

"I never suspected Mercy cared about me one bit," Frank mentioned. "She's always been quiet around me."

"Not quiet, shy. There is a difference, Frank." Holly collected their plates. "Now, how about we take a walk to the school for dessert? The children are expecting everyone to show up and take a look at their art work and they've decided to sing a few songs, too. It will be exciting."

Frank pushed his chair back, pulling the napkin from his lap. He placed it on the table, offering to help clean up.

"No, you are my guest. I'll clean up quickly. I think we should go and make sure not to miss the children's presentation."

Frank and David went out on the porch while Holly cleared off the table. It was late in the evening and yet the day had not ended. Light still filtered in from the clouds. Tall pines left shadows on the street but it wouldn't get dark for at least another hour.

The three hurried up the street to the school house when a joyful song rose up from the open windows of the large structure. A combination of children's voices, along with the teacher's guiding voice had the three anxious to get there. "We don't want to miss any more," Holly called, pulling her husband's hand. Frank's long legs kept up with them and he was soon standing in the back of the school room as the children's chorus sang away.

Mercy was near the front, holding hands with two small girls. They looked shy and afraid until Mercy began to sway back and forth, guiding them along. Her voice rose above the rest, it's beauty and clarity not lost on the crowd. Everyone looked to watch her belt out the song.

Frank was mesmerized. He didn't know Mercy had such a wondrous voice. But then, there were a lot of things he didn't know about her or had even tried to get to know. Shame began to wind its way from the back of his head to the tips of his shoes.

She had been here all along and he had pretty well ignored her for years even though deep in his heart, he knew she was the one he wanted. A surge of anger went through him. He had wasted so many years that he wasn't sure if she'd want him after all this time.

Holly said she loved him, too. Was it true or was she assuming? Maybe it was time to find out. He didn't want to scare her off with another kiss and lose any real chance of telling her how he felt.

He'd have to convince her that everything he said was the honest truth. When the music was over and everyone clapped so hard to show their appreciation, the guests were told to help themselves to dessert. Frank stood in line with the everyone else, waiting his turn to be served.

He stood in the line where Mercy was handing out cake. When he stood in front of the table and reached out his hand, hers connected to him by accident. She looked up and blinked several times. "Oh! I didn't know you were attending our social. Thank you for coming."

Frank grinned. "Did you make this?" It looked identical to the cake she had given him as a welcome home gift.

"Yes," she offered shyly. Then, more boldly, "Didn't you already have cake today?"

He laughed out loud and picked up a fork. Taking his time, he put a piece on the fork and lifted it to his mouth. "Yes, I sure did and it's so good I want more."

As he spoke, he looked intensely into her bright violet eyes. They were so different than any color he'd ever seen. Mercy's were violet, like a dainty spring flower and her red hair made her look unique and beautiful as far as he was concerned.

She clearly did not know how beautiful she was. He was going to make it a point to let her know, but she was opening her mouth as if to say something. He was entranced as he focused on her sweet smile.

"Doctor Mason, there are others behind you!" Her words were spoken quietly enough but one of the children called out.

"Doctor Mason! Doctor Mason!"

Frank looked away in order to get a hold of himself. He side-stepped out of the way, excusing himself and moving to the back of the room. He stood against the wall, embarrassed that she caught him staring so. Well, at least she'd know how he felt. But, was it too late?

Sheriff Knight and Deputy Will stood beside him, eating their sweets as well. The three watched the others from the back of the school while enjoying their goodies.

"I'm here for the desserts," David mentioned, stuffing another huge bite in his mouth.

"Me too," Deputy Will said. "There's cookies with icing on top. I'll be back." He pushed off the wall to get more sweets.

The sheriff laughed. "Can't keep him in shape. He's ten years younger than me and twice the size. When I was that age, I didn't have a gut the size of a barrel."

Frank laughed. "I recall you had some baby fat on you."

"Yeah, when I was ten. Deputy Will needs to cut back on the sweets. You can't tell him a thing though."

"Cupid will hit him on the head sooner or later and he'll drop weight like a squirrel running for a nut that fell from a tree."

"You think so? As long as he can do his job, that's all I care about. Don't want no outlaws getting away from him if he can't keep up."

Frank shook his head. "Send him to Old Doc Roberts for a physical."

Sheriff Knight laughed out loud. "If he's not *fishing.* Hope tells me he is there maybe two days a week any more. She's lucky to be working even though I told her she can stay home."

"Two days a week? What do the residents do for the other days?"

"If there's an emergency they know to go find him at the lake, or cottage. He has a small camp right outside of town. His housekeeper goes with him."

Frank was surprised. "Mabel?"

David nodded. "She's still his housekeeper but we all know what's going on. He doesn't try to hide it."

"No kidding?"

"Doc told Hope they're too old to get married and he doesn't care if they live in sin, he's in love and that's all that is important."

"Doesn't he realize it's her reputation to worry about, not his?"

David shrugged. "She doesn't seem to mind. You know the folks here. Everyone has some quirks and we don't judge like they do in the big cities. I guess they all feel the same way about the doc. As long as he does his job, no one is complaining."

"Good for him. He's been single for a long, long time. He's dedicated his life to this town." Frank wondered if he'd ever be able to stay in one place long enough to feel that way.

It wasn't long before the children began to leave, some complaining until they were led outside by the stern voice of a parent. The sheriff stayed to make sure everyone got home safely so Frank stuck around, determined to walk Mercy home.

When she was packed up and ready to leave, he went to her. "Do you mind if I escort you home?"

She looked around to make sure he was talking to her. "If you'd like to. You don't have to though."

He didn't understand why she'd say that. "I want to, Mercy and I 'd be obliged if you'd say yes."

She nodded. "Yes."

As they left together, he was going to make it clear that he had one intent in mind and that was to make Mercy his wife. If she'd have him.

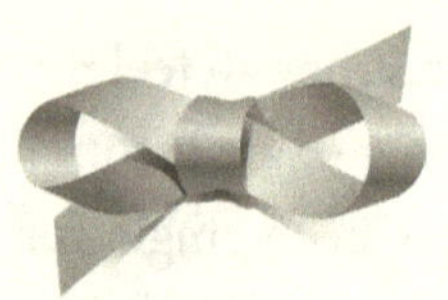

Chapter 3

MERCY WASN'T SURE WHAT Frank's intent was, but she liked the company on the way home. Sometimes it was darker than she liked when she was on her way, even though nothing dangerous ever happened in Belle. It was a relatively quiet town. Except for last year when the bells were stolen. That was another story, though.

She was content to walk beside him, not speaking. It felt pretty natural to have him here. They had known each other since her family moved here when she was about eight years old. She knew almost everyone in town except for some of the newer residents. "Do you ever miss them?" she asked.

"My parents?" He nodded, immediately knowing who she meant. "I do. I want to go visit their grave before I leave."

"You're leaving?"

"Not for awhile. Sooner or later, I have to accept a position somewhere. I didn't go to medical school to come home and be idle."

She understood. He was probably anxious to get started. Mercy sighed. There was no sense getting herself in an uproar over him. He wasn't planning to stay. She had to be strong enough to accept his friendship and not fall in love.

It was probably too late not to fall in love.

She didn't remember a time she didn't love him.

But now, she had to let him go. It was time to make peace with the past and move forward. Maybe even marry someday. Yet, the thought of marrying someone else made her stomach upset. She placed a hand over it.

"Are you ill?" he asked.

Why did he seem to notice every little thing about her. "No. I probably did too much today after just getting over a cold." At least that would give her a good excuse if she had to get away from him. Feigning sickness was a valid and appropriate excuse, wasn't it?

He tucked his arm through hers. "Let's make sure you get home safely," he told her, his voice stern. The shock that went through her at his touch made her even more woozy. By the time she got home she'd be so dizzy, he'd have to carry her inside!

It didn't happen that way, of course, but he did walk her to the door and when she looked into his eyes, she knew he was going to say something. Did she want to hear what he had to say?

"Mercy, I came home because I had to make things right."

"From what I understand, you did. Holly and David appreciate how you stood up and asked for their forgiveness."

"How did you know?"

She didn't know what to say. Everyone was talking about it. "I heard it mentioned at the school before the dessert social."

"Did that town gossip stand at David's door listening to me? I came straight from the stage to the sheriff's office."

She shook her head. "No, I believe she mentioned she was walking down the alley and accidentally heard you when she walked by the kitchen window this evening on her way to the school."

It was spring, the signs of warm weather stayed well into the evening. A window or two open sent a breeze through the homes this time of year. It didn't surprise him that their voices carried outside. But, the sheriff's home was beside an alley and she happened to be walking by? Frank sighed. "I'm sure she accidentally heard my words."

Mercy laughed. "Well, let me see if I can recall the order of things. Lucy Mae told Charity when she went to the café, who told Natalie's grandmother as she was dining there. Then, Ruth Winslow from the boarding house came in to buy some sweets and was told. From there, Mildred at the newspaper found out, and low and behold the teacher Grace Winkleman mentioned it this evening. I overheard everyone talking about you."

His eyes were filled with humor. She felt quite bold when he gazed at her and she couldn't help but smile back. Before she realized what he was doing, Frank lifted the back of his hand and ran it down her cheek. She ached to lean into it but knew better. This was not going to help her when he left.

She turned away, reaching for the door knob. "Goodnight, Frank."

<> <>

"Wait, Mercy! Did I say something or do something wrong?"

It was time to explain. "Frank, you left here to go to medical school engaged to Holly. You're back now and will leave someday, probably very soon. I'm not sure why you are attaching yourself to me, but I honestly don't think you should. Goodnight."

"I didn't want to marry Holly! It was a foolish mistake when I promised her mother I'd take care of her. I didn't mean I'd marry her, I meant I'd help to look out for her, you know, like a good neighbor. In her will, she had written it differently and I didn't have the courage to discount a will! I'm sorry, Mercy, it was you I've loved all along!"

He was standing facing a closed door. She had already gone inside. Had she heard anything he said? He knocked on the door, then turned when he heard a voice from the street.

"Everything alright there, son?" One of the neighbors from the end of the block stopped.

"It's fine. I had to escort Mercy home as she wasn't feeling good."

"Thank you, son. I guess I should call you doctor now."

"It's fine, sir. I don't need to be called doctor in my home town."

"Have a good night now," he told Frank, standing there while Frank took himself off the porch and started across the grass. He turned back once to see the man and his wife waiting until Frank opened his own door and went inside.

He may be from this town, but there were some here that still didn't trust him. Especially now that his name was being mentioned all over town thanks to that gossip. He ran a hand through his hair, took off his jacket and went back outside to sit on the front porch.

Except there were no chairs outside to sit on. Standing by the porch railing, he gazed over to Mercy's home. It was dark except for one small lantern glowing through the upstairs window. Her house was neat and tidy, the rows of flowers along the side starting to bloom. Pink, lavender and yellow colors were hidden by the darkness of the night. Frank knew they were there. Every single year those same flowers had sprung up. He remembered looking at them while he waited to see when Mercy left her house.

Why hadn't he ever mentioned to her that he was interested? He shook his head, shoving his hands deep in his pockets. Leaning back on the balls of his feet, he stared up at the night sky, its tiny stars peeking through the darkness. It sure was beautiful here. Not like the city.

He had missed home. The last four years had been hectic and rough and he barely had time to look up and enjoy city life. He thought he'd want to stay there and become a surgeon someday.

Yet, standing here made him realize he'd be content living his life out in Belle.

If he had someone to come home to. He glanced up at her window again. It was now dark but he swore there was a slight movement, unless the curtain caught a light breeze. Except, there was no breeze this evening.

Frank's mouth turned up slightly before he turned in for the night.

Maybe there was hope after all.

. . ∞ . .

< > < > < >

FRANK WOKE TO THE HARSH sounds of banging at the front door. "Doctor Mason! We need some help!"

He quickly got dressed and ran downstairs, buttoning his shirt as he swung the door open. Mercy and another woman stood alongside a small boy, no older than ten. She was holding his hand and steered him inside.

"What's going on?"

"This young man fell and the doctor is away. Can you help him?" Mercy asked, begging him with a look of desperation.

There was no way he'd ever be able to refuse her. "Of course! Let's get him on the kitchen table and see what's wrong." Frank scooped him up, now seeing that his arm was wrapped.

A whimper came out of his small mouth. His mother tried to comfort him. "It's fine, he is a doctor."

The boy stared at Frank aster he set him down and began to unwrap the cloth.

"Are you really a doctor?" he asked, his bottom lip trembling with fear.

"Yes, I am. What's your name, young man?"

"Carson."

Frank noticed the paleness of his skin. He didn't want the boy passing out. "Well, Carson. What do you want to be when you grow up?"

The boy shrugged. "I'm too little to know."

Frank tilted his head, trying to get the boy's attention away from the bloody cloth. "When I was your age, I wanted to fish all day and night and catch the biggest fish ever."

The boy's eyes got huge. "You did?"

"I sure did."

"Did you ever catch it?"

Frank had been concentrating on the boy's arm so hard he looked down to find Mercy had filled a bowl with water. She set it alongside the boy on the table and handed him a clean cloth, then answered for him. "I don't believe he's ever caught the biggest fish," Mercy added, smiling at the tear-stained face.

She gave Frank a concerned look. The boy's arm had been sliced open and the blood didn't want to stop. He shook his head slightly to let her know she didn't have to worry. Frank looked at the boy's mother, whose face was paler than her sons. He nodded to Mercy who looked for a chair and helped her to sit. "Let's give the doctor some room to work," he heard her say.

Carson's big brown eyes were on Frank. He sighed, knowing the boy was about to hurt more. "It looks like you sliced your arm pretty good, young man. How about we put some stitches in there and make it better?"

"Will it hurt?"

Mercy took his other hand. "It may hurt a little, but I'll be right here to help you get through and then you'll feel so much better."

Carson looked at his mother first until she reassured him it was okay. He stared at Mercy for sometime before blurting out, "You have bright hair!"

The tension in the room softened. Frank was threading a needle while Mercy spoke to the boy, trying to keep his mind occupied. He wondered if she knew how good of a nurse she made?

At the first stitch, Carson cried out but Frank had no choice. If he didn't stitch the boy's arm, he'd bleed to death. That wasn't going to happen in Belle. He tried to help calm the little fellow. "Carson, would you like to go fishing with me?"

His eyes widened? With pools of tears in his eyes, he nodded, his lower lip puffed out. "Can she come, too?" When Frank looked up, he watched how the boy was hanging onto Mercy's hand.

"Yes, if she wants to." He had to put another stitch in and concentrated on doing his job. He smiled when he heard Mercy say she'd be happy to go fishing with them.

After putting in several more stitches, he cleaned the area and wrapped it good in case the boy got it dirty. His mother had finally come to her senses and kept thanking Frank.

He held up a hand. "It's fine, ma'am. He must keep the bandage on until I can take a look at it next week."

"I appreciate all you did for him, Doctor Mason."

Frank knelt down again and looked Carson in the eye. "You have to take good care of the arm. Do what your mother tells you and make sure to never take off the bandages until we can do it together. Can I count on you?"

Carson nodded, his little head flopping excitedly.

Frank roused his hair. "Okay, son. When you come back next week, if everything looks good, we'll plan to go fishing the following day. Is that a deal?"

"Yes! It's a deal!" He started to jump up and down until Frank realized he needed to secure the arm better.

"Hold on, Carson. Let me get you a special bandage to wrap around your shoulder. It's called a sling and it's important you leave it be. Your mom can take that one off at night."

Ten minutes later, the two left Frank's house a little less fearful. He even heard Carson giggle at something Mercy told him.

"What did you say?" he asked, cleaning up the mess on the table. She helped, gathering the excess bandages.

Mercy giggled. "I told him the biggest fish you ever caught was no bigger than his little pinky!"

Frank shook his head. "Now you know that's a lie, but I'll thank you now for keeping him calm. He has a pretty deep gash on that arm. Any chance you know how he got it?"

"Did you see Martha's cheek?"

"I was too busy to notice, but her face was scrunched up and tears flowed when I did get a chance to look up. Her face was so pale I'm glad you sat her down, else we'd have two patients."

"Her husband packed his things and took the only wagon they had and left Belle. Before he left, she tried to convince him to leave the horse and wagon. She was arguing with him when he backhanded her and she flew against a table. Carson saw what happened and attacked his father with a knife. Except it was turned on him instead."

Anger hit Frank at the thought of a young boy trying to defend his mother. "Carson is lucky. It was a sharp knife."

Mercy nodded. "He is brave. It's why I agreed to go fishing. He's going to need all the distractions he can get right now. His mother as well."

"You have a heart of gold, Mercy. Thank you for bringing him to me."

"I knew if we tried to take him to Doc Roberts outside of town, he may bleed too much."

Frank placed a hand on her shoulder. It wasn't meant as anything more than a kind gesture. "You did the right thing. The cut is deep and he *was* bleeding too much. I'm afraid he never would've made it to Doc's cabin."

Mercy plunked down on the chair. She lifted a hand and pushed her hair back. "I'm sorry, I must sit a spell. This has all been quite exasperating."

Frank checked her pulse. Her skin was slightly pale, but her cheeks were flushed. "I think the enormity of what you did just occurred. I am quite impressed, Mercy. You'd make a fine nurse."

She fanned her face. "I never gave any of it a second thought. Knowing you were here made my decision to bring them to your house easy. I knew you would help."

Frank sat down in the chair opposite her. His hand reached across the table. "It felt good. Thank you for trusting me."

"I'll always trust you, Frank, er, Doctor Mason."

He squeezed her hand. "It's Frank, please. We're friends and I'd like to keep it that way. I always want you as my friend, Mercy. Are you willing to be friends?" He wanted so much more. Yet, the thought of her shutting the door on him again like she did last night was too upsetting to think about.

If he wanted her love, he'd have to be her friend first.

Chapter 4

•• ❧ ••

FRANK HAD GONE TO FIND Doc Roberts while she came back home to gather some supper for Martha and Carson. She was certain the mother was too emotionally exhausted to make a decent meal.

Quickly gathering fresh vegetables from her bin, she chopped them up and added them to the beef and stock she had simmering on the stove. Mercy had started the broth early this morning when she had gone out to work in her garden. After adding potatoes, she had a nice, thick stew going. While it was cooking, she cut a loaf of fresh bread, wrapping half in cloth to take to Martha's house. At least they'd get a good supper.

Mercy busied herself around the house, dusting and sweeping the floor, even though it had been done the day before. She kept hearing Frank's voice in her mind saying how she was the one he had always loved. She had been standing behind the door when he had proclaimed his love. Her heart had pounded so fast and loud she figured he heard it on the other side of the door.

She had heard every single word he had said. The good thing was she had waited so long to hear him declare his love for her and then when he finally did, it was through a door. To hear it through a thick wooden door was not how she had wanted to know about his true feelings.

On the other hand, Mercy knew if he left again, she'd be heartbroken and that was the one thing she wanted to avoid. She looked up at the ceiling.

Is it too much Lord, to ask for your help to figure this out? Do I forgive him or keep him at a distance? Do I love him back as much as he claims to love me, or wait? I need your help and guidance.

Mercy spent most of the afternoon confused. She really needed an answer. At the same time, Frank didn't know she had heard every word he proclaimed. Maybe she'd let him think she hadn't heard. Wasn't it safer that way?

Besides, he said he wanted to be friends.

The soft knock on her door pulled her from her sour thoughts. When she answered, Frank stood there, a fistful of fresh picked flowers in his hand. He held them out to her. "I thought if you were taking supper to the boy and his mother, she'd like some flowers to go with the meal as well."

Mercy was impressed. At first she thought he was going to present them to her, but remembered his words about being friends. So, friends it was. "It certainly will make her feel better. I'm getting ready to take their supper over. Would you care to walk along?"

Where did that come from? He waited on the porch, but asked, "What can I help you with?"

She hurried to the stove and scooped soup into a smaller pot, then placed it inside a large basket. Tucking the bread alongside, she covered everything with a cloth and handed the basket to Frank. "I'm ready if you are."

They walked down the street, turning onto Main. Most of the residents had already gone home to their families for the evening. The street was almost empty except for Sheriff Knight who was stepping down from the porch at his office. He tipped his hat and waved.

"Evening, Sheriff," Frank called out.

"Evening, folks. I heard what you did," he called out. "Thanks for taking care of the boy. We'll all help to keep an eye on things there."

"We're taking some supper over to them so Martha doesn't have to cook," Mercy told the sheriff. She turned to Frank. "Do you think her husband has truly left?"

He shifted the basket from one hand to the other. "I'm afraid he's long gone. Town gossip said he's been having relations with one of the hotel's maids. He picked her up at the far end of town and left Belle for good."

Mercy was shocked at the recent news. "That's terrible. Poor Martha! She really needs us now."

He agreed. "She'll need to find some work to keep going. I've been thinking about asking if she'd like to work for me. Especially after the conversation I had with Doc Roberts today."

Mercy stopped. "Oh? Are you going to tell me what was said?" She gazed into his eyes, which were lit up with excitement. Her curiosity was getting the best of her and it seemed as if Frank was dragging the conversation on purpose.

He grinned. "Well, the doc wants me to take care of Carson until he's healed since I was the doctor who fixed him up. He's asked me to take over a few days a week to take the load off of him. He's thinking to retire in the next few months."

"Since he's barely in his office any more, it may be a great opportunity for you."

"I haven't decided where I want to work yet, Mercy. I came home instead of taking an offer at a hospital in Philadelphia to tie up loose ends and decide what to do with the family home. I'm torn between the city and a more quiet atmosphere. For now, I've agreed to open up three days a week."

Hope began to surge through every single nerve ending. Was this an answer to her earlier prayer? Was Frank going to become the next town doctor? Even though Doc Roberts was still working a few days a week, he was considered the town doctor. Many folks waited for him to come back and the mornings when he was in, they lined up in front of his building waiting for him. They trusted him.

But, most of all, was there a chance for Mercy and Frank? She gave him a genuine smile. "I'm glad you'll be here for awhile," she told him, feeling shy all of a sudden.

"Thanks, Mercy. So am I. I'm considering opening shop in my home instead of his. The place is way too much for one person. I can set up a temporary office in the parlor."

"If you want to give Martha work, hire her to help you get it set up. I can help, also."

Frank turned to her and took her hand. "I'd like you to be my nurse. You're very good at it, you know."

Mercy was surprised he'd offer her a job. "You want me to work for you?"

"Sure, what's wrong with that?" he asked, an incredulous look on his face.

"I'd never thought about being a nurse. Or, considered having a job."

Frank sighed. "I know you don't need the money, Mercy. Your parents left you a sizeable inheritance, but I could really use your help."

He was right. Her parents had thought ahead to provide for her when they unexpectedly died a few years ago, leaving her the house and a sizeable amount in a bank account. Her father had been fortunate in the early days of gold mining and saved the money he made. But first, her parents had been fortunate enough to travel around some before settling in Belle.

Mercy didn't have to worry about a job, but she did volunteer several times a week. She loved visiting some of the older folks and help them in their gardens or doing things around the house.

If she took the position it meant she'd be around Frank quite a bit. Would it be enough time to convince him that Belle was where he belonged? He said he came back because she was the one he had always loved. And yet, now he was offering her friendship. Confusion racked her soul.

What was stopping her from telling him she heard what he said? Maybe she wanted more. Mercy knew it was time for him to prove himself, to show her in some way his words were true. What better way than to find out how he truly felt by working alongside him? "I'll do it. Yes, I'll help. I'll still need to visit with a few townsfolk on a regular basis, but I can do that on my days off."

Frank gazed into her eyes, mesmerizing her. Mercy was the first one to turn away. "We better get the basket to Martha before she starts her own meal."

Frank took her by the elbow and continued to walk. They had been standing in the middle of the street. She turned to see a few people watching them. Mercy grimaced. She hoped they hadn't heard the conversation, otherwise the news would be all over town in less than five minutes.

She gazed down the street to make sure the town gossip wasn't prowling around. Satisfied, they went to Martha's front door and knocked. It took a few moments for Martha to answer as the door opened slightly. "Can I help you?" the soft voice called out.

"Its Mercy and Doctor Mason. We've brought you a basket of food for supper."

The door swung wide. Of course Martha had to be cautious. She had to be terribly afraid he'd come back and try to hurt them. After what he had done, Mercy hoped the man had gone far away, never to return. A small part of her wanted something terrible to happen to him in return even though she shouldn't feel that way about another human being.

"Won't you come in and sit a spell?"

Mercy knew from looking at the dark circles under Martha's eyes, she was being polite. "We can't stay," she piped up before Frank had a chance to answer. " I have a pot simmering on the stove, but we wanted to make sure you got something to eat. It's been a long day for the both of you."

"I truly appreciate your kindness." She gave them a weary smile that didn't quite reach her eyes.

"We'll say goodnight then."

"Wait!" Frank lifted a hand. "I was wondering if you would like a job, Mrs. Winslow. I'm going to be operating my services from my home and am in need of some help. Would you care to stop down tomorrow afternoon to go over details?"

Mercy thought it was a brilliant way to ask her by not giving her a chance to say no. She blinked a few times as if she couldn't believe what she was hearing. "Is this truly a job, doctor?"

Frank smiled. "Yes, it is. I need to have the parlor fixed up and ready by next week and then I will need it thoroughly cleaned several times a week. Germs, I've learned, is the number one cause of many sicknesses. Cleanliness will help keep them at bay."

"I understand. I will be needing a job. Thank you, kindly."

"We'll see you at one? You are welcome to bring the boy if you don't want to leave him here."

"That'd be fine. Goodnight, Doctor Mason. Mercy." The woman closed the door on them.

Martha and Frank looked at each other and laughed. The moment they did, the wooden door swung back open. Martha reached out and took the basket from Frank. "I forgot this," she said, her smile so wide Mercy thought her face would crack open.

When they left, a lightness she hadn't felt in years encircled Mercy. "It was so kind of you to offer Martha work. She seemed delighted and she's going to need it."

He looked back at her house. "It looks like she may need more help than we realized. There's a shutter hanging crooked on just one hinge. It doesn't look like her husband was too fond of working."

Mercy grunted. "If you listen to gossip you will learn he mostly frequented the saloon and a few other establishments. He didn't spend much time tending to his home. Or, his family."

"That's too bad. If I had a boy like Carson, I'd be doing whatever it takes to give him a happy home."

"I'm sure you would. Carson really likes you, Frank."

"I like him, too. Don't forget, you will be going fishing with us next week after his check-up."

"How can I forget?" She placed her hand through his arm. "Especially since I'm pretty sure who will be reeling in the biggest fish!"

Frank grunted. Under his breath he muttered. "We'll see about that."

Mercy smiled to herself. It was going to be an adventurous day for certain. She was really looking forward to spending some time with him at the creek.

It didn't take long to turn the corner onto Tall Pine Lane. Frank dropped her off at her porch, his face lit up from their conversation. "Thanks for a great day, Mercy. I'll see you tomorrow. Can you come over and help at one also?"

"The day isn't over yet, Frank. I have plenty of supper to share. Why don't you come in and join me?"

Frank looked up and down the street. "It isn't appropriate to be in your house alone with you, I'm afraid."

That's when Mercy noticed Mr. Bright and his wife a few doors down standing behind a smaller pine tree, peeking through the thin branches, watching the two of them. "Oh, dear. I see we have some folks watching us. They may try to start some terrible gossip. Hold on, Frank! I have an idea!"

She didn't wait for his answer, but hurried inside. She remembered how years ago her parents had set up a small table outside on the porch each Sunday afternoon to partake the noon meal and enjoy the fresh spring air. The table had been buried by books and whatnot for many years. Mercy worked quickly, placing the books on the floor and dragging the small table through the door's opening.

"What are you doing, Mercy? Let me help." She felt his strong hands on her shoulders. Giving up the effort, she moved away to let him pull the table the rest of the way through. He set it on the porch, along with both chairs that were already outside.

"That's perfect!" She clapped her hands with glee. "I'll be right out," she told him before dashing inside to dish them each a bowl of delicious stew. Carrying the bowls on a large platter, along with fresh bread and churned butter, Frank took them and set a bowl at each place setting. After several trips, the table was completely set and he helped her into her chair.

"Thank you," she said, breathless. "We work good together, don't we Frank?"

He nodded, placing a cloth napkin on his lap after he sat across from her. "That makes me feel good about our future together."

She looked up quickly. "What, uh, what do you mean?" she asked with a nervous laugh.

He had already begun to take spoonfuls of the stew and place them in his mouth, eating heartily. After chewing and swallowing, he grinned. "As a doctor and nurse working together. What else did you think I meant?"

43

Chapter 5

Mercy was late! She had gone to see old Hank Parley at the edge of town. He lived alone in a large house and had no family around to help him. He was so grumpy most people steered clear, tired of his tirades and mean words. All except for Mercy. She had fallen in love with his rough exterior and worked hard to make him laugh despite his misery. Every now and again she saw the corners of his mouth turn up.

One of the reasons she thought he was so miserable was because he was hurting. She noticed some of the fingers on his hand were starting to curl up on him, causing his hand to look deformed. Mercy had mentioned it to Doc Roberts but he didn't think there was anything to do for him. The doc said that was the meanness popping out.

Mercy made a mental note to mention it to Frank. Maybe he'd be able to check his medical books and find something to ease the poor man's pain. She came around the corner and then ran to Frank's front door, knocking loudly.

Frank answered right away, a look of concern on his face. "Is everything okay, Mercy? You are extremely late. We've been waiting on you for some time now."

"I'm so sorry." She pushed a strand of hair back before letting out a puff of air. Her pulse was racing so hard it felt as if it'd pulse right through her skin. "I was visiting with Hank and didn't realize what time it was."

"Old man Parley! I hear he's gotten so miserable no one will talk to him any more."

Martha waved and gave her a smile while Frank ran a hand through his hair.

"I go see him so the rumors are not true."

Frank nodded, still a look of concern on his face. A small crease ran across his forehead. She hadn't noticed that before. "Sit down, Mercy."

Mercy joined Martha at the table, sitting alongside of her. "Hello, Martha."

The other woman's hands were clasped in her lap. Mercy felt compassion for her, she was so nervous. It was probably from living day to day in fear of her husband. Thank the Lord he was gone. Mercy made a vow to help her in any way she needed. *Dear Lord, help me to be a good friend.*

After listening to Frank explain the roles both women would be playing in his practice, he asked if there were any questions. "If not, I'll see you both at seven sharp tomorrow morning. We may as well get this room in order for next week's patients."

"I have some time now, Doctor Mason. If you'd like, I can start today."

Frank nodded. "That's fine. Where is Carson?"

"One of the lovely ladies from town is sitting with him. Holly, the sheriff's wife, offered to attend to him today. She said since the doctor has practically put her out of a job, she needed to spend her time doing good deeds. I was happy for the help."

"Holly is a kind person," Frank told her. He turned to Mercy. "Do you want to start today also? It's fine if you have other plans."

"We are a team so I'll help all I can," she told him, giving him encouragement. She was supposed to visit with Thomas Rider today, but was glad to miss the visit. The man kind of made her feel uneasy anyway. The last time she was over to help with his flower beds, he got way too close, brushing against her arm with his and lingering there. He had offered to make lemonade and tried to talk her into going inside. Luckily, the next door neighbor stopped in at the same time so they sat on the back porch having a cool drink instead. Mercy was reluctant to go back over again this afternoon and now she had a good excuse not to. She wanted to be courteous and let him know. "I must quickly run down the street to Thomas Rider's house to let him know I'll help with his garden another day."

Frank tilted his head. His gaze moved slowly to her hands, which were twisted together. She hadn't realized she was behaving so peculiarly. The thought of Thomas did make her worry, especially since the last time she was there. He was a strange neighbor who had only moved into the neighborhood this past month. Everyone was trying to be kind to him since he seemed all alone in that house that needed so much work. Several people had already offered to help him. It was what the townsfolk did, help each other.

"I can go tell him if you want to help Martha," Frank offered.

Relief that she didn't have to face him today surged through her. Mercy was grateful. "If you don't mind. Let him know I'm helping to get the office opened up, so I'll help with his garden soon."

"Certainly. Thank you, ladies. I appreciate the help." Frank walked to the front door, then turned around, his eyes on her.

"Was there something else, Frank?" she asked.

He shook his head, then turned around and left.

Martha stood. "We better get started."

They gathered strips of material and a bucket to wash down the walls of the parlor. There was thick dust on shelves of bookcases and around the edges of the furniture, causing a cloud of dust in the air when they wiped it down. Frank had set a bottle on the counter to add to the wash water. He mentioned it will help sanitize the room.

Pouring some of the disinfectant in as instructed, the women got busy wiping down walls. There wasn't much furniture in the parlor any more. Mercy remembered it being wall to wall settee's and chairs in here. She wondered if Frank had given things away to someone in need before he left for medical school. He had the same type of kindness inside of him that Mercy did. If she saw someone needed something, she'd do whatever she could to help them.

It was refreshing to know Frank was still the same, even after being away four years. "Frank told me yesterday that Doc Roberts will be dropping off some medicines and supplies to get him started. The doc should be here within the hour," Martha told her.

"I'm excited for this new venture, aren't you, Martha?"

"I'm scared to death. I've never been on my own before." The woman brushed a curl from her eye.

Mercy gave her a hug. "It will all work out. You are not alone, Martha. The town of Belle will make sure nothing bad ever happens to you again. We'll all help you as much as we can."

"I appreciate the kindness, believe me. No one has ever done so much for me before."

Mercy smiled, dipping her rag in the bucket. "Well, that's why you wound up in Belle. We all help each other no matter what. And there may be a time someone needs your help as well. I'm glad you are here. Doctor Mason will be a good employer to you."

Mercy just wondered if the same doctor would be a good employer to her?

<><><>

Frank strolled a few blocks down the street until he came to the old mansion. The yard was overgrown with weeds on one end, while another side was cleared away. A small garden enclosed by a black wrought iron fence abut two feet high encased several rows of vegetables that had been planted recently. Some of the plants were weeded out while the other parts still needed done. This must've been what Mercy was working on.

The atmosphere around the property felt as eerie as a story Frank once read as a child. Tall pines stood towering over the back of the property line while overgrown bushes and trees grew throughout the yard. Frank took a few steps at a time, noticing how the wooden stairs creaked under the weight. No wonder Mercy was nervous when she mentioned this place.

The door flew open the moment he knocked as if the man was expecting someone. He was probably waiting on Mercy. Then Frank looked into his eyes and saw anger flash when he realized it wasn't her. At least that's what Frank thought. The man gave him a look of utter surprise. "May I help you?"

"Are you Thomas Rider? I'm here for Mercy."

He looked about, back and forth, even more surprised she hadn't been standing in his yard. "I'm Thomas. Where is she?" he asked, a desperate note in his tone.

Frank stepped closer, perusing the man. There was something off about him, although he wasn't able to pinpoint what. Frank had studied psychology in medical school and every single aspect of what he learned had him drawing the conclusion this man wasn't right in the head. He knew right away this man was not to be trusted and he was surprised no one in the neighborhood had noticed. That was unusual for Belle. "My name is Frank Mason. Dr. Frank Mason. I'm opening a practice to help Doc Roberts a few days a week and Mercy is going to be my nurse. She wanted you to know she can't help you today." *Or, any day if I have any say in the matter!*

Another flash of anger crossed Thomas Rider's eyes before he tried to hide it. "Do you know when she will be able to come back?"

Frank hesitated. He didn't want to lie to the man, but he didn't want Mercy coming back here, ever. "I'm not sure. I have a lot of work to do to get the office ready. It will be awhile before she can help her neighbors again."

"Do you mean a few days? A few weeks? What exactly do you mean?" he asked, his tone of voice sounding almost desperate.

Frank leaned in. "I do not know, sir. But, I will tell you this; Mercy means a lot to me. We've been neighbors for a long, long time. I'm right next door to her and I care deeply for her well being. I just want to make that clear."

He didn't wait for the man to say anything since it looked as if he would argue with Frank. His training told him to assert himself and move on. That's what he did. Stomping across the yard, he went through the gate, closing it behind him.

The man called out. "You can't keep her from coming here."

Frank swung around. "She's going to be working. I'm sorry she'll have to help you another time. Is there a problem with that?"

The man raised a fist and shook it. "I mean it, Doctor Mason. You can't keep her from me."

Frank kept walking. She was not going back there. He wasn't going to mention their conversation to Mercy, but now he knew he had to. He swung towards Main street to talk to the sheriff first.

David Knight was busy speaking with a tall woman so he waited outside until she left. When he said hello, she looked terrified before nodding to him. He went inside to find David and the deputy discussing the last visitor.

"She wasn't sure who it was but thinks someone has been watching her house."

Frank caught the last part of the conversation. "Where does she live?"

"Oh, hey Frank. That's Mrs. Smith, one of your neighbors on the far end of Tall Pine Lane. Lost her husband a few years back and lives alone with her two children. Have you noticed anything out of place on your street since you returned?"

"I think I may be able to solve this mystery. Mercy has been helping the man that moved into the old mansion, Thomas Rider. I volunteered to let him know she won't be coming today since she's helping Martha get my office up and running. He seemed frustrated and upset that she wasn't going to be there. His beady eyes were darting all around looking for her and he told me I can't keep her away from him. I thought that was unusual."

"That a fact?" the sheriff said, standing up from his desk and staring out the large window. "Why would he get upset? The neighbors have been helping him with the yard. Mildred has taken him some baked goods a few times."

"I don't know. I got a bad feeling when I was there. I don't want her going back."

"A man's tuition is nothing to frown upon," David told him. "We'll be keeping an eye on him. Do you fear Mercy is in danger?"

Frank shrugged. "I can't rightly say, but I know he was upset that I showed up instead of her. I'll keep close watch on her to make sure she goes nowhere near that place. I let him know she means a lot to me."

The sheriff nodded. "Thanks, Frank. If you keep an eye on Mercy, I can concentrate on keeping watch on Mrs. Smith's house.

Perhaps it's time to make a house call myself, let him know we're watching his every move. Nobody gets away with crime in Belle."

Relief went through Frank's whole body as he walked home. The sheriff was tough. He didn't put up with any nonsense. It made a man feel good about his home town knowing the law was doing its job.

Now all he had to do was convince Mercy she needed to listen and stay away from that mansion. He knew she liked helping others, she always had. She was the perfect nurse.

She was the perfect woman.

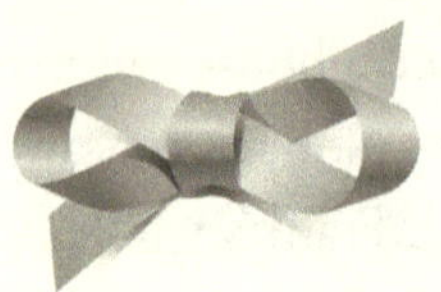

Chapter 6

Frank seemed to be taking a long time to speak with Thomas Rider. She turned to Martha who was finishing up the last wall. "Don't you think Frank's been gone awhile?"

"Doctor Mason? I hadn't noticed." Martha watched her reaction and then smiled. "Oh, Marcy. You like him, don't you?"

She had never revealed to anyone her feelings for the doctor. Martha was so kind and seemed like the type of person that didn't judge others. "I think I do."

"You think so? Well, you either do or you don't, Mercy. There's no in-between with love."

She sighed, pushing another loose tendril from her brow. "I suppose you can call it love then." She glanced up to find Martha smiling and shaking her head. "What is so funny?"

Martha picked up her bucket and the pile of rags. "I believe the good doctor may have the same feelings, dear. He seems enamored by you. I've caught him staring at you when you aren't looking."

Martha's words made her blush. "Even so, I worry that he will leave here when he finds the right position. So, I don't want to tell him my true feelings. Even though he did mention something the other night about me being the one for him."

"What!"

"Well, through a closed door. He doesn't know I heard him."

"You haven't told him you know how he feels? Oh, Mercy! He is clearly in love with you. What are you waiting on?"

"I'm not sure. It's a long story."

"Well, I've got plenty of time. We'll talk tomorrow since your doctor is back. I see him coming down the street."

Mercy looked out the window and watched Frank swaggering down the street like he owned Tall Pines Lane. She gave Martha a quick smile. "He sure does have the looks, doesn't he?"

"If you like his type," Martha laughed. "I best be heading home to Carson."

Frank came inside, a frown on his brow. He nodded to the ladies before looking around the newly washed parlor. "It's starting to smell so much cleaner in here. Thank you, ladies."

"I must be getting back home to Carson, Dr. Mason. Is there anything else you need from me today?"

Frank shook his head. "Not that I can think of. We'll start again at seven sharp tomorrow morning. You can bring Carson if you need to. I have plenty of books to keep him occupied."

"Thank you, sir. I may have to do that." The door closed softly when Martha left. Mercy gathered up the bucket and took it out back to dump the water. When she came back inside, Frank was still standing in the same place, staring at the wall of the far side of the parlor.

"Is everything okay, Frank. You look perplexed."

He turned to her, a serious look on his face. Was he going to fire her? Already? She put the bucket away and wiped her hands, worried now that she did something wrong.

"We need to converse, Mercy. Do you mind taking a seat."

"Certainly." She sat on the edge of the settee in the parlor. Frank sat beside her and took her hand. *Oh dear, here it comes! He's been gone all afternoon. What did he want to tell her?*

"You're not going to be pleased when I tell you this, but I had to go see the sheriff today."

Relief struck her like a fast moving winter storm. "You're not firing me, then?"

He smiled. "No, Mercy. I'd never fire you."

"Will you tell me what is wrong?"

When Frank looked into her eyes, she realized he was deeply concerned. "I went to speak with Thomas Rider and his reaction to you not coming today has me worried about you ever going back there."

The moment Frank mentioned Thomas Rider's name, her shoulders tensed and she began to bite the inside of her mouth. "What did he say? Or do?"

Frank hesitated, as if he didn't want to tell her at first. "He was angry that you hadn't shown up today and informed me that I can't keep you away from him."

Her hand flew to her throat. She felt her pulse thumping away below her fingers. "He makes me very nervous," she admitted.

Frank tensed. "Has he ever done anything inappropriate?"

"He kept inviting me inside, but I always refused. Then he'd brush his arm against mine."

"He touched you?"

"No, it may have been an accident. We were working side by side." She didn't' want to accuse the man if she wasn't sure. How would she know unless she went inside and that she wasn't about to do.

"Did it make you uncomfortable, Mercy?"

"Very much so," she admitted. Maybe she should not have told him. The look in Frank's eyes worried her. They were on fire.

"I promised the sheriff I'd keep you close and watch your house. I'm afraid he's going to be busy watching a neighbor's houses since Mrs. Smith complained someone was snooping around her place last night."

"Oh! Do you think it was him?" This wasn't good news. From the feelings she got when she was at the mansion, Mercy swore she'd never go back there. "I'll never go near that man again. Do you think he's watching my house, too?"

"I don't think he has been."

Mercy gave him a look. How would he know? "We can't be sure though."

"I can. I'm the only one watching your house at night, Mercy."

"Oh!"

"I wake up several times during the night to wind up staring out my window. Your house is right in my path of sight. I'd know if someone watched you." He took both her hands in his. "Mercy, I care for you so much. I want you to know how much you mean to me. We've been neighbors for so long and I've ignored you for years growing up, but all I wanted to do was study and read. I'm sorry for not paying more attention to you."

Mercy was surprised at his admission. She gave him a nervous smile. "I forgive you, Frank. We are friends now, after all."

He brought his handsome face closer. "Is that all you want from me, Mercy? Just to be friends?"

Dare she admit how she felt? Did she tell him she already knew he admitted how much he cared for her? She took a deep breath and held it in for a moment, contemplating what to say next. She closed her eyes, unable to look him in the eye for her next admission. "I heard you through the door, Frank. I heard you say its always been me you loved."

The room went quiet, not even the breeze through the window made the curtain flap. Mercy was afraid to open her eyes. What if he had changed his mind?

A deep guttural sound came from his chest. He lifted both her hands and placed them in his. "Mercy, look at me. Open your eyes."

Her lids fluttered open. When she saw the way he was watching her, those deeply intense eyes filled with a warmth she couldn't decipher, a tear slid down her face. She wanted to swipe it away but he had her hands in his and wouldn't let go. He leaned down and kissed her hands, one at a time and then pulled them along with his to his chest.

Frank leaned in to kiss her. He hadn't said a word, nor did he have to. The love he felt for her was truly showing in his eyes, on his face and Mercy felt like she was going to drown in them.

She moved her mouth to his, letting herself feel his kiss for the first time. It was raw and beautiful and she felt truly loved for the first time in years. A shudder went through her. Frank broke the kiss and wrapped her in his arms. "I'm sorry if I caused you any pain. I've wanted you forever, Mercy. Trust me in saying this, whatever choice I may make, I won't leave here without you." He took her face in his hands and she gazed into his eyes. "I promise."

"Frank, I've loved you forever." Her whispered words caused him to pull her closer.

He groaned and kissed her again. She wanted to tell him more, but he kept kissing her, not letting her get any words in for some time. Then he broke the kiss and told her exactly what she wanted to hear. "I love you, Mercy. I wondered if you heard me that night."

It took her a moment to compose herself after his proclamation of love. "I did, but honestly, Frank, knowing you were leaving again had me upset."

He brushed a tear away. "I won't leave you. Ever."

"It's hard to believe you, Frank. I do understand how you felt obligated to Hope's mother and the misunderstanding about the engagement. I forgive you for that part. But, leaving for four years without telling me how you felt hurts so much inside. I want to believe you'd never leave me again, I do."

He pulled her into his arms. "I want to show you, Mercy. Perhaps I found what I was looking for right here. In Belle. Can you be happy with a country doctor?"

She looked up, confused. "What do you mean?"

He smiled down at her, a twinkle in his eye. "Doc Roberts mentioned he may retire real soon. Seems he's found love after all these years with his housekeeper Mabel. Belle will need a good doctor to replace him."

She grinned. "Would you be happy here?"

He nuzzled her neck. "Only if you are here with me."

She shuddered again, not believing this was actually happening. "I am speechless, Frank. Totally speechless. Why, just last night you were talking about being friends, and now? You proclaim your love for me like this and I'm not sure what to do. Not that I'm complaining. No sir, I'm more than happy to hear the words I've longed to hear."

"And I'll continue to say them." He let go of her hands and stood away from her. Mercy watched in anticipation as he went down on one knee. "I'm serious enough to ask you this. Mercy, will you marry me? A country doctor who doesn't have much to give you, except my love?"

Mercy got down on her knees as well so she could look him in the eye. She flung her arms around her future husband. "I will," she promised and pulled his face closer. When their lips met once again, she whispered how he just made her the happiest woman alive.

He kissed her again, then helped her up, holding her hands in his. "I want you to tell the whole town of Belle we are getting married, dear Mercy. Tell everyone, tell the newspaper, shout it so loud the tallest pine tree will sway with glee."

She threw her head back and laughed out loud. "I think everyone will know in about twenty five seconds. I just spotted our nosey town gossip walk right by your window. Oh, look, she just turned around. Here she comes."

A knock on the door prompted the two to separate, knowing they were being inappropriate. Frankly, Mercy no longer cared. She was going to become Mrs. Frank Mason!

Frank opened the door just as Lucy Mae swept inside, not waiting for an invitation. "Hello, Miss Jackson, what can I do for you?" Frank's voice was amused at the way the town gossip burst through the door. It made Mercy hide a small laugh.

"Well, I've heard rumors that Thomas Rider is bothering the ladies of this town and I'm here to find out the truth. Is it true, Doctor?"

"I'm afraid I can't divulge any information to you, Miss Jackson. I will say he is under investigation and perhaps you should go talk to Sheriff Knight."

She puffed air from her lungs and placed a hand on her hip. "Well. I certainly have done that and he refuses to divulge any information as well. He told me to stay away from Tall Pine Lane and not to discuss what I know with anyone. That'd be fine and dandy if I had something to discuss!" She pointed a finger at Frank. "I did see you leaving the sheriff's office a short time ago. So, when he refused to tell me anything except warn me from being on the streets at night, I decided to take matters into my own hands and come to you. Besides, no proper woman would be on the streets at night by herself."

Mercy was getting a headache from all the noise the woman was making. Her huffs and puffs and shaking finger was making Mercy's head pound. "Please, Lucy Mae. Don't be judging the doctor. He is going to be helping the sheriff solve this case, but you must be absolutely quiet and not tell a soul they are watching Thomas Rider discreetly."

Lucy Mae walked over to where Mercy stood. "What exactly are you saying, Mercy?"

Mercy looked at Frank. She was going to tell the woman the truth. Sort of. "Word has it that Thomas is a bad man and it's just a matter of time until the sheriff catches him at what he is doing. So, you need to stay clear of his house and anywhere he may be at. Can you make sure nobody goes to help him, Lucy Mae? No matter what? It is important he doesn't find out what we are doing or he may run away and then he'd never be caught. If you can do this, you'd be helping to solve the case."

She clapped her hands together. "Yes, I'll make sure the other volunteers do not get fifty feet near him." The excitement in her voice had Frank rolling his eyes.

"A hundred feet," Mercy told her.

"What? Oh? Okay, I'll make sure no one gets one hundred feet near him."

"Okay, Lucy Mae. I'm glad you are on-board. I'm counting on you to help us. Can you report back here next Tuesday? The doctor's office will be open then. Just don't let anyone know what you are doing."

Lucy Mae was nodding her head up and down so hard she was sure to have her own headache before the day was done. Mercy gave the town gossip a hug and whispered. "Thank you for keeping this quiet."

After she left, Frank looked at Mercy with surprise. "Do you honestly think she is going to keep that quiet?"

Mercy shook her head. "Part of it she will. Lucy Mae will be so busy bragging to everyone how she is in cahoots with the sheriff and the doctor on a mission that everyone in town will know in about one half hour. Then, after that she will be so busy watching to make sure no women go to Thomas Rider's house, we won't have to worry about her at all."

Frank looked impressed. "You know how this town operates quite well. You'll make a wonderful doctor's wife."

"Yes, I do and I will."

He followed her gaze to her hand, then picked it up and brushed a soft kiss across her skin. "I'm going to the jewelry shop now. Would you care to come along and pick out your ring."

Mercy looked at him aghast! "Choose my own ring? I've never heard of anyone doing that."

"We can do as we please, my soon to be wife." Frank pulled her along. Closing the front door, he steered her down the street towards Main Street where the only jewelry shop in town was located. It was getting later in the afternoon, so they hurried to make sure to get there before the owner closed shop for the night.

As they walked down the street, she saw a shadow from the corner of her eye. Had someone been watching them?

Frank noticed her tense up. "Is anything wrong?"

"I thought I saw something move quickly in the neigbors yard."

Frank stopped. He turned completely around, perusing the area. "I don't see anything. Are you sure?"

"I suppose I may be a bit nervous since you mentioned how Thomas Rider was watching that other woman."

"That's it! We're exchanging vows as soon as the preacher can marry us. I don't want you alone one more night."

Even though she tried to stay calm and act as if she wasn't scared, Mercy's heart pumped so fast with each hidden corner they walked past. The more fearful she was, the more she imagined someone watching them.

Frank kept his eyes opened and kept reassuring her no one was following them. Even the sheriff had rode past with his gelding, patrolling the streets. She was being silly and overacting, digging her fingers into Frank's arm a little too hard.

He placed a hand over hers. "Mercy, don't worry. We are all watching out for this man. He's not going to hurt anyone, I promise." His words gave her immediate relief. He knew how worried she was.

"I wish I'd have never gone there to volunteer my services. The first time he allowed me to help with the garden, I felt uncomfortable. But, I just thought I was doing my duty to help others."

Frank patted her hand. "Now, don't you worry. Let's go get you a fine wedding ring and see if we can't get married."

Mercy looked at Frank, shocked. "I didn't realize you meant today!"

He laughed. "Of course I mean today. Right now, in fact. I can't bear to be apart from you one more night!"

Chapter 7

"I'm sorry. Pastor Elkins went to visit some church members who moved to Laramie. We don't expect him back until Sunday morning for church."

Disappointment shook Frank to the very core. How was he going to protect Mercy if he wasn't with her each and every night. "Can you send a telegram and have him come back early? We'd like to marry as soon as possible."

The deacon looked affronted. "Sir, I am sorry, but the pastor deserves a few days to visit his family. You'll have to wait until he returns." With that, he closed the door to the parsonage.

Mercy began to shake. Her shoulders shook so hard, he was starting to get worried. "I'm so sorry, Mercy. I tried. Listen, I'm not going to take this lying down." He turned and raised a fist to the door, prepared to knock again.

She reached out her hand. "No! Frank! Please, don't!" When he truly got a chance to look at her face, she was trying so hard not to laugh. Her cheeks were bright pink and her eyes were filled with unshed tears. They were about to overflow and run down her cheeks. She let out a burst of laughter. Mercy hadn't been upset at all!

Frank grinned then threw back his head and laughed out loud. The parsonage door opened a tiny crack. "Everything okay out here?" the man asked.

Frank waved him off, taking Mercy's hand and guiding her down the stairs. "I'm so sorry, Mercy. I got out of hand. We can wait a few days until he comes back."

"If it makes you feel any better, Frank, I'll ask Martha and Carson to stay with me. That way neither one of us are alone."

"That's truly a smart idea. Let's take a walk to her house and see if she'd like to come over now."

Mercy took his hand as they walked down the street. She smiled at him, her eyes lighting up. "You are becoming quite overprotective, Frank. We are being stared at."

He turned to see some of the other townsfolk watching them, a few with big smiles on their faces. "We're getting married!" he announced. Well, he shouted it so loud the sheriff looked up as he passed them again.

"Congratulations are in order," the sheriff called out. His grin was almost as big as Mercy's smile.

"Thank you, Sheriff Knight," Mercy said. She gazed at her hand, then slid it in the folds of her dress.

Frank watched her closely. He realized he was so prone to keeping her safe, he neglected to get her a ring. That way no one would mistake his intent for her. "I'm so sorry, Mercy. Let's go see what the Jeweler has. You need a ring this moment."

They walked into the only jewelry store to find the perfect ring for his bride-to-be. Frank waited patiently while the jeweler showed her several ones that were a bit too high for his pocket book. Even so, he was going to make sure she had one she liked.

Mercy spotted a smaller stone set in a plain band in the last row. "That one," she told the man.

He looked surprised. "That little thing?"

"Yes, please."

The proprietor placed a magnification tool against his right eye after he pulled the ring from the shelf. It was evident he wanted to sell a larger stone. He looked up at her, aghast. "Are you certain you want this one?"

"I'm positive," Mercy whispered, sliding the ring onto her finger. She looked at Frank, her innocent eyes staring into his own. He almost took a step back at the sweet desire and love emulating from them. "It's perfect."

Frank nodded to the jeweler. "We'll take it."

"It's not what I'd recommend, sir."

Frank ignored the jewelers constant groans while he paid for his purchase. He was good at letting someone whine and then doing as he pleased. It helped him deal with patients many times in medical school. When he was an intern and he'd go on rounds, patients complained to him more often than not. He learned to keep a listening ear, but at the same time he knew what the patient truly needed.

They left the store, the small bell jingling as they stepped onto the boarded walk. "Now you have proof that we will be married," Frank told her. "No one can question our intent."

"Thank you, Frank. I'm still in shock that you want to marry me."

He placed a hand on her shoulder and turned her towards him. "Look at me, Mercy. I wanted to marry you a long time ago. I hope someday you will believe me."

She shook her head. "It no longer matters, does it? We have the rest of our lives now."

Someone coughed behind them. The hairs on the back of Frank's neck stood up. When he swung around, Thomas Rider was leaning against a gas lamp post, hands firmly across his chest. He was glaring at Mercy. Then he spoke up.

"Mercy, when are you going to help me with my garden?" His voice was so loud many heads turned to stare.

"Keep walking, Mercy. He shouldn't be shouting at you on the street." The man was clearly upset and quite brave to call out to Mercy in front of others. Frank knew his diagnosis of the man was correct. There was something not right in the man's head.

"Mercy! When are you going to help me?" His angry voice rang out loud and clear.

Sheriff Knight was riding his gelding down the street at a slow pace until he saw how everyone was watching them.

When Thomas snapped his head around to find the Sheriff coming towards him, he quickly moved away, staring a hole into Mercy's back. Frank didn't miss the look of deranged anger on his face.

"Everything under control, here?" Sheriff Knight leaned down, his eyes on the man walking away even though he was talking to Frank and Mercy. Thomas Rider turned a corner and crossed the street.

"So far, Sheriff. Thomas called out to Mercy. He was angry so we tried to ignore him."

"That was the right thing to do. It's time I had a one-on-one with him." The sheriff tipped his hat and took off in the same direction as Thomas.

Frank knew when David got riled, he was no one to mess with. It was time to deal with the man any way and he had faith the sheriff would take care of things. Frank was a doctor and he fixed people, not hurt them. But if anyone tried to hurt Mercy, he'd be the first one to go after them, doctor's oath or not.

They knocked on Martha's door a few blocks away. After explaining the situation, Martha agreed to stay with Mercy for the remainder of the week. "I'll stay as long as necessary. Hopefully, when the pastor gets back, he'll perform the ceremony right away, and that man will stop bothering people. After what I've been through, I'm well armed these days." She nodded towards a rifle sitting alongside the door, an easy reach for her if someone came in uninvited.

Frank nodded. "Thank you, Martha. You surely are a big help."

"Let me gather some things for Carson and I. Please come in while I get what we'll need for a few days."

Carson was pleased to be staying at Mercy's house. He began to bounce up and down until his mother reprimanded him. "It's hard to keep him still," she told them.

Frank laughed. "In a few days the stitches can come out and we'll go fishing as promised," he told the boy. "In the meantime, you'll have to follow the rules and try not to get too excited."

"Yes, sir," he told Frank.

As the four of them walked back to Mercy's house, Carson's little hand found it's way into Franks. He was shocked at first and even pulled back for a second before realizing the boy was showing him trust.

Mercy gazed at him and the boy. Her sweet smile made his throat constrict. How did he ever think living in a big city would be better than what he had right here?

<><><>

When Mercy saw Carson take Frank's hand, she almost stopped dead in her tracks. What a humbling sight it was. He was so adorable with a tiny sling on one arm and holding the doctor's hand with his free one. She imaged their children through the visual image she saw. He would make an excellent father.

Things had changed so rapidly. Mercy didn't think she'd be able to forgive him at first until she realized love was all that truly matters. It didn't really make a difference what happened in the past. The past was meant to be forgiven. They had right now and she was going to make the best of things.

Losing her parents had made for a solitary life in the big house where she lived. Even though they had provided for her, she was lonely. Her philanthropic works helped, but there had always been a void. Now she knew that void had been Frank.

"A penny for your thoughts?" His whispering in her ear had her blushing.

"I'm finding out my void was you."

He shook his head. "What was that you said?"

She giggled. "Oh, nothing. I'm happy you came back home, Frank."

He leaned in to speak in her ear again. "Me too. I can't wait until Sunday."

"What if the pastor can't marry us on Sunday?"

Frank shook his head. "That is not a possibility. I'll tell him if he doesn't marry us, we have to live in sin. Then I'm sure he'll get the job done."

"So, are you saying it is a job to marry me?" She looked up at him, her eyes sparkling. Frank was not much of a joker. He was a serious doctor who needed to relax and laugh more. He was the kind of man who got things done in an orderly fashion. He liked to be in charge and move mountains.

Today seemed quite different, even with the upsetting incident earlier. Mercy was surprised when Frank looked at her and piped out, "Ah, Mercy! We can't get married. I already have a job, and two jobs is way too much for me to handle."

She was going to retort back, but instead burst out laughing at his remark. Soon, the four of them were walking towards Mercy's house laughing so hard a man grumbled from behind. Mercy looked back to see Old Man Parson walking down the street, his cane keeping him steady, although steady to him looked awfully wobbly.

She stopped to let him catch up. "Mr. Parson! I'm so happy to see you out in the sunshine."

"Where do you see a sun? There's nary a ray of sunshine in that miserable sky!"

"Well, sir, it depends how you look at things. Would you care to walk with us?"

"I'm fine as dandy by myself."

Mercy knew how to handle him. She'd be sweet and kind no matter what he said. If it got out of hand, she always reminded him she spoke to him because she wanted to and that usually softened him a bit. He was such a sour apple at times. "I'd like to introduce you to the new doctor in town. This is Dr. Frank Mason. He'll be standing in for Doc Roberts a few days a week."

Frank held out a hand. Parson lifted heavy lids to stare point blank at the doctor. "A doctor, eh?" The old man's shaky hand reached out to meet with Franks. Mercy let out a small sigh. That was a relief. At least he was being slightly cordial today.

"Yes, sir," Frank told him, using a loud even voice. Right away Mercy realized that her husband-to-be knew how to deal with old, grumpy men. He had even raised his voice to accommodate the man's loss of hearing.

"Well, you got a bunch of patients here in town who say they're sick, but they just take time away from those who are. Be careful, doc, or you'll be treating people without ailments."

Frank nodded at his advice. It was almost as if he was truly paying attention to the old man's every word and taking him seriously. "Thank you for the tip. As a physician, I noticed your hands, Mr. Parson. I believe I have some ointments that may give relief to those knuckles that look painful. May I come over in an hour to give you an examination?"

The old man was clearly surprised that anyone took an interest in his wretched, crippling fingers. He was quiet for the first time since Mercy got to know him. This was highly unusual. "Mr. Parsons, I'll come along if you'd like. I'm going to be Doctor Mason's nurse."

The old man stared at her. "I'd say you're more than his nurse." He shrugged bony shoulders. "Sure. Why not see what this young quack can do."

Mercy looked at Frank trying not to grin.

"We will see you then." Frank held out his hand again and this time the man gave it a good shake.

He nodded to Frank. "Don't be late!" he grumbled, right before he walked off in the direction of his home.

Mercy watched him shuffle his feet. "I'm sorry about the name calling, Frank. He's a bit voracious with words."

Frank held out his arm for her to take. "No need to worry. I've heard worse in my four years in medical schooling." As they walked he told her some stories of terrible patients at the hospital there.

When they got to Mercy's house, she showed Martha and Carson where to put their belongings. It would be nice to have the company, she thought. Although, after Sunday, she hoped to be married and living with her husband. She hoped the pastor felt the same way and didn't try to get them to wait to marry. With Frank's tenacity, she was pretty certain he'd talk the pastor into marrying them on the spot.

A smile slipped across her face.

Things were finally falling right into place.

And she was falling more and more in love with the man who always had her heart.

Chapter 8

"Martha, will you be okay here for a few minutes? I want to go with the doctor to exam Mr. Parson."

While Martha worked in the kitchen to start the makings of supper, Frank and Mercy went to see the old man. They had to walk by the mansion, so Frank instructed her to stay close and not to look towards the house.

Frank noticed Deputy Will was on his horse, tucked away in a small alley off of Tall Pine Lane. He was relieved to know the sheriff was doing something about the threat. They were taking it seriously and had a man watching the old place.

With Martha and her son staying with Mercy, and now Thomas being watched, Frank was able to relax his mind to concentrate on his job. He tried to hide how worried he was for Mercy's sake. Frank had looked into Thomas Rider's angry eyes. He wasn't right in the head. Last year Frank had to do an apprenticeship at The Institute of Philadelphia Hospital for the insane. It was a large farm and they had spent every single day there for two months. He felt like he knew a little bit about the insane from that one experience.

The sad part was many of the patients weren't really insane. Frank had tried to speak with other doctor's about his analogy, but he didn't get too far. Most of the elderly were put there since they were poor and had nowhere to go. He had met grumpy men like Mr. Parson who were in pain, not demented.

The worst of the patients, the ones who were truly insane, had the same look in their eyes as Thomas Rider. Empty. Cold. Evil. He pulled Mercy closer. They had to get rid of this man who was now living in their town.

But, how? Can they throw him out for shouting at a women in town?

Will the women's claims hold up in front of a circuit judge? Even if they did, that may be a year from now until one came through their small town. Where would this man go? To another town to create havoc for others?

Frank knew it was his duty to examine the man and proclaim him insane to get him off the streets of Belle. He would speak to Doc Roberts about it when the elderly doctor came into town on Saturday.

"Here we are," Mercy said, pointing to old man Parson's house. The old man was sitting on the porch waiting.

"Just what I suspected." He pulled a stop watch from his pocket, his hand shaking worse than before. "You're late!"

Frank held out a hand. "Better late than never. Shall we go inside and take a look at those hands?"

Mercy helped him up, holding onto his arm as they made their way inside. Frank noticed the old man had a decent view of the whole street from his window inside. He had the old man sit at the table while he did a thorough exam. "That's quite a view you have."

Parson nodded. "It is if you're interested in what's going on outside, which I'm not!"

Frank almost laughed. He took the old man's wrist to check his pulse. "Ever see anything strange going on at the old mansion?"

His pulse quickened, which was interesting since he just said he had no interest in looking outside. Which meant he did look outside all the time. He probably had nothing better to do since it was probably painful to move much at times.

"The times I do have to look out, the only strange thing I see is the owner. He's an odd bird."

"He is that," Frank agreed. "Will you do me a favor and let us know if you see anything odd or anyone there that shouldn't be there?"

The old man nodded. "Heard the gossip in town already, doc. Wish my hands didn't hurt so much, I'd fire my old six-shooter at him the next time he stands on the edge of his property staring at the ladies that walk down the street. Although it hasn't happened in a day or two. Guess that's 'cause everyone knows he is a snake in sheep's clothing."

Frank looked at Mercy to find a surprised look on her face. She spoke up. "Mr. Parson, that's the most I've heard you say in a long time."

It's because they were making him feel needed. Just asking him to keep an eye on his next door neighbor gave the old man something important to be a part of. Frank opened his medical bag he set on the table when they first came in and took out a tin. "I'm going to put some of this on your hands for now. It should give you some relief right away."

"What's that, doc? You get that from one of those traveling medicine shows? It looks like something that quack had when he came through last year, selling wondrous nostrums for female complaints and other gregarious nonsense!"

Frank tried not to laugh at the old man's choice of words. "I promise you it isn't from a traveling medicine show. This is liniment for Rheumatism and Catarrh." Frank showed him the lid.

"C-a-t a- what? I can't even spell that word let alone say it. I'm pretty sure I don't have that!" He pulled his hands back.

Frank reassured him. "Mr. Parson, Catarrh simply means an inflammation, mostly from congestion."

"Are you sure?" He squinted at the tin and looked sceptical.

"I assure you." Frank wondered what he'd say when he gave him some Willow Bark to chew on. He rubbed the ointment on his knuckles where the worst of the arthritis was. "If you do this twice a day, it will give you some relief. It's not a cure, but along with the Willow Bark, you'll start to feel better."

Frank pulled out a small sack with several pieces of the analgesic.

The older man's eyes got huge. "What in tar-nation is that?"

"It's Willow Bark. You chew on it. I promise it will relieve the pain."

Mr. Parson shook his head, letting out a big laugh. "Chew on it! You are a quack! Your ointment is soothing my hands but now you have me chewing on tree bark! You may be worse than old Doc Roberts!"

Frank didn't budge from his treatment. "I promise you will feel better. We have to go, but remember what I said. Chew on that when your hands get to feeling bad and rub the ointment on tonight before you go to sleep. I'll be back to check on you tomorrow." With that, Frank closed his medical bag and nodded to Mercy. He knew it was time to leave quickly before more questions were asked and the man would reject everything.

They made a quick exit. As they walked back to Mercy's house, her shoulders began to shake again. When Frank looked at her, the laughter in her eyes had him letting out a burst of laughter as well.

They passed the mansion, not even bothering to look that way. They were still laughing at the old man's reaction to modern medicine.

When they got back to Mercy's house, Martha had supper ready. Frank ate heartily and enjoyed his evening. They sat on the porch with some lemonade Mercy had made earlier in the week.

He hated for the night to end. Martha and Carson had gone to bed. Frank stood. "It's time for me to go, Mercy. Thank you for a lovely evening." With that, he wrapped her in his arms and placed a gentle kiss on her mouth.

She sighed.

He took in a deep breath.

"I can't wait until Sunday," he murmured, stepping away. "Go on inside and lock up."

He hated to remind her she wasn't safe outside by herself as the serene look on her face fell. "I almost forgot about that man."

"I know, but we can't forget. I'm afraid he is a danger to you and other women. I believe the Sheriff is taking care to make sure he doesn't bother anyone."

"How will he do that?"

" A good, old fashioned talking to, I assume." Frank wasn't sure it would be enough.

"I hope so. Good night, Frank."

"Good night, Mercy."

Her soft voice stayed with him even while he watched through his window during the night. If he had to stay up until daylight, he was going to make sure Thomas Rider didn't bother her. Ever.

<> <> <>

FRANK HAD GONE TO SEE Mr. Parson first thing in the morning. The ladies were still setting up his shop, doing last minute preparations for when it opened on Saturday morning. Doc Roberts was planning on stopping in when he returned from an extended fishing trip with his housekeeper Mabel.

When the townsfolk found out Frank was opening his own practice, several townsfolk stopped in to make sure they would be able to be seen. They didn't believe it until they saw it with their own eyes.

"I'm amazed how many people stopped in today," Martha announced. "It's like a door that never closes today."

"Everyone is just curious." Mercy was trying to keep her mind on her work. It was so difficult because hopefully Sunday would be her wedding day. She had been secretly working on fixing one of her good gowns to walk down the aisle. She even made a thin veil for her hair.

Martha stopped what she was doing and stared at Mercy.

"What?"

"I don't believe you have your mind on your job at all, do you, dear?"

"Oh, Martha! I'm so excited and scared at the same time." She put down a vial of laudanum Frank instructed her to keep on the top shelf. "What if I don't please my husband? I'm not sure what to do."

The other woman gave her a reassuring smile and a hug. "The love between you and the doctor is so strong that no matter what, it will all work out. It's a natural thing that occurs and you can't be frightened of it."

"Still, it worries me."

Martha smiled. "I wish I could reassure you that it's a wonderful experience, but I did my duty and produced my son. At first, my husband was sweet and kind and I enjoyed the marriage bed with him. Later, when he began to drink more, it was awful. I'm not a good person to discuss these things with."

It was Martha's turn to be hugged. Mercy held her for some time until one of the neighbors started towards the doctor's house. "I'm so sorry you had to go through what you did, Martha. I will pray you will find happiness with someone soon."

She shook her head vehemently. "There's no way I want another relationship. Ever! My son will be enough for me. Now, let's see who is here now."

They spent the rest of the day putting finishing touches on the office to open first thing in the morning. Tomorrow would be a busy day. Even so, Frank kept finding patients along the route from Mr. Parson's house who claimed to need help right away. He had made three house calls by the time he got back in the late afternoon.

"I think we are going to be quite busy tomorrow," he noted, sitting at the head of the table. "Mr. Parson is almost out of his ointment, too. I promised him I'd stop after the office closes for the day."

Mercy looked up from her plate of leftover chicken and dumplings from yesterday. It was easier to heat it up since they had so much to do. "Seems like an awful lot of ointment to use up so quickly."

Frank shook his head. "Mr. Parson had the idea to double the dosage since I told him twice a day. He figured if he put it on four times, it would work twice as fast."

Mercy grinned. "I believe we have our hands full with Mr. Parson."

Frank agreed. "I told him I'll make one more trip there and then he has to come to the office for more. That way he will walk every day. Part of his problems can be solved if he is more active."

"Getting exercise sounds reasonable," Martha chimed in.

She had almost forgot Martha and Carson were sitting at the table. Her eyes had been on Frank ever since he got in the door.

An idea arose. She wanted Martha as her next door neighbor when she married Frank. "Martha, I'd like it if you stayed on at my house after my marriage to Frank. Aren't you renting your house from Chester Reynolds, our banker?"

Martha nodded. "I was worried about paying the rent since it is due soon. I only have half." Then she burst into tears. Frank was quiet while Mercy gave her a hug. When the woman was done sniffling, her son slipped from his chair and hugged her waist. "It's okay momma. Don't cry."

She quickly sobered, making sure to give her son a great smile. "I'm sorry, Carson. I'll bet you are excited about going fishing next week."

His head bobbed up and down and his good arm went in the air as he pretended he had a fishing pole. They all laughed to change the mood.

Mercy took her new friend aside. "We'll work out details later, Martha. I'll help you move all your things early in the morning and get you settled here. I promise you won't be charged an arm and a leg. Plus, now you have a true job and can pay your own bills. This is truly a wonderful life."

Martha smiled but it didn't reach her eyes. Mercy knew she was worried and didn't blame her. It had to be hard to be all alone to raise a child. She was grateful her parents left her some money in the bank or she'd be in the same situation.

Frank sat on the porch with her later that evening before he headed home for the night. "It's such a clear night, Frank. Look at the stars peeking through the trees."

"Shall we take a short walk."

They walked to Main street and back, enjoying being the only ones out. The sheriff's office was closed for the night. Mercy glanced toward the mansion when they got back on Tall Pine Road but it was dark inside. She didn't want to think about that man tonight.

Frank dropped her off at her front door, reminding Mercy to lock up behind her. She gave him a sweet kiss and waved goodnight. From the corner of her eye she thought she saw a shadow and then discounted it when she looked again to see nothing but a small bush in her neighbor's yard.

"Everything okay, Mercy?" Frank was attentive to her every move. She was glad he was going to be her husband.

"I guess I'm still not quite back to normal after the Thomas Rider scare. He hasn't bothered anyone today and I swore I saw a shadow, but it turned out to be that bush over there."

Frank ordered her to stay inside while he investigated. She didn't listen but peeked her head around the corner of the door while he crossed the yard. When he came back with the good news no one was out there, she felt quite silly. "I'm sorry. I guess it's time for me to get some sleep."

"You have been working hard these past few days. Good night, Mercy."

"Good night, Frank."

Chapter 9

Saturday morning went so fast. Mercy worked alongside Frank as he saw one patient after another. Around one in the afternoon, Martha put a sign on the front door. She came back in and ordered the two of them to sit down. "I closed for one hour. Come to the table and eat some dinner."

Mercy was so hungry she ate everything on the plate. When she did look up, Frank was staring at her, smiling, when she realized he had been speaking to her.

"I'm sorry, Frank, I'm just so hungry."

"You have a good appetite, Mercy. That makes me happy to know you'll stay healthy and strong. Just what a doctor's wife needs."

She gave him a look. "I honestly don't know if that is a compliment or you are teasing me."

He reached over and lifted her chin. "It is a compliment. I love everything about you."

Mercy blushed.

"Thank you for giving me this chance to redeem myself, Mercy. I was so worried you'd reject me."

"There's no need to worry, Frank. You make my head spin and my heart do triple beats. I'm helpless when it comes to you."

"Child in the room," Martha interjected when Frank took her hand and began to kiss each fingertip.

Mercy pulled her hand back, giggling. It happened every time he was in the room with her. She'd forget about anyone and everyone else. Luckily, it didn't happen when they were seeing patients.

Carson giggled from his seat at the table. "I think Doctor Frank was trying to eat your hand."

Mercy burst out in laughter. "Oh, Carson. That's silly. I think the doctor was being funny."

After that, the afternoon flew by. Mercy swore everyone in town stopped by, including Doc Roberts. He was impressed with the clean office and commended Frank on a well organized operation.

The moment the last patient left, Martha went outside and flipped over the open sign. "We've had a good day. I'm glad you are not open tomorrow, Doctor Frank."

Mercy smiled at Frank's new name. The townsfolk had been calling him Doctor Frank all day. Somehow it fit. "Tomorrow is Sunday and we will be getting married if the pastor agrees."

Frank nodded, taking off his jacket he wore while in the office. "It feels good to get that off." The moment he hung it up on the peg by the door, someone began to knock furiously.

Mercy ran to the door when someone shouted. "The stage coach was robbed. There is a man hurt terribly! Doctor Frank, can you come help? Doc Roberts sent me to get you."

Frank put his jacket back on and grabbed his black bag.

Mercy gathered some rags in case they'd need them. "Do you want me to come with?"

Frank shook his head and pulled out a tin of ointment from his coat pocket. "No, Mercy. I need you to take this tin to old man Parson if you don't mind. I'll send the deputy to go along with you to be safe."

Mercy and Martha cleaned up the area while waiting for the deputy. When he finally did get there, he left his gelding tied to the post on the front porch.

"I'm here to escort you to old man Parson."

"I'll be right back, Martha. Do you mind going next door to start supper? I'll be back as soon as I can."

Martha went next door while Mercy and the deputy went the opposite way. Mercy wasn't paying too much attention since her mind was on the tragedy at the stage office. "Do you know what happened, Deputy Wills?"

"There was a robbery and they killed the stage coach driver. We don't have much detail except the man inside was left for dead. Somehow he drove the stage back before he slumped over dead in the middle of town. Sheriff and I dragged his limp body to Doc Roberts house then sent for Doctor Frank. Not sure if the man will make it. Too much blood."

The deputy was walking so slow. She kept going ahead of him, then slowing down to wait. The tall pines were leaving shadows as the sun went down. She wanted to get Mr. Parson his ointment and go to Frank in case he needed her nursing skills.

Mercy slowed again when she realized the deputy had been dragging his feet again. It was time to move him along or they'd never get back in a timely fashion. "Deputy Wills, we should try to .."

She swung around and stopped short. The deputy was not behind her. A small sob escaped her when she saw two feet sticking out from behind the pine tree. Had he fallen? She ran to the tree only to feel a hand against her mouth, restraining her from yelling out.

"Do not scream."

Thomas Rider! Mercy was strong but this man had a grip on her arms and she tried to get away. She swung a foot and almost caught him in the leg until he placed a rag over her mouth. Dizziness surged through her and her vision became blurred. He watched her, his evil eyes boring into her. With trepidation Mercy realized he was using ether to put her to sleep. She tried to get away, even attempting to bite his hand but the cloth was held too tight.

She heard a shuffle as if someone were coming upon them. "Put her down or your dead," a wobbly voice called out. She knew that voice. It sounded like Mr. Parson. Her mind wanted to try to protect him but her body was starting to shut down.

Fear encased every single bone in her body until she didn't care any longer.

<><><>

FRANK RACED DOWN MAIN Street towards Doc Robert's house. There was a flurry of activity going on with the sheriff standing on the porch holding up his hands. He was trying to calm the ever growing crowd out front.

"Let the doc through!" People moved over for Frank to get through when they saw him coming with his black bag. This was probably the most excitement the town of Belle got to see except for the time when the bells had gone missing.

"Where is the patient?" he asked David.

"In there. Doc Robert's is working on him."

Frank left the crowd standing outside, refusing to answer the questions that were being thrown out there. He wasn't able to answer anyway since he didn't know anything. When he pushed open the door, Mabel the housekeeper was holding a bloody rag against the man's shoulder. She looked horrified, even though he was sure she'd seen things like this before.

Doc Robert's looked up and nodded. "Good! Good! You're here. Go on Mabel, let the young man take over."

Frank shrugged off his jacket and assessed the situation. The man was still, his breathing labored. "What happened?"

"Not quite sure, son. Looks like he was shot at fairly close range."

"Is the bullet still in his shoulder?"

Doc Robert's shook his head. "Can't tell until I get some of this blood cleared up."

The man on the table groaned. "You going to talk all night or fix me up?"

Frank looked at Doc Roberts and grinned. The stranger had gumption. He held the cloth tighter against the open wound to try to slow the bleeding. "Going to have to look at the other side, mister. Can you turn on your side?"

The man worked hard to move, gritting his teeth and demanding a shot of whiskey to take away the pain.

Doc Roberts tried to reassure him. "I'll give you something to help the pain." He instructed Mabel to get his morphine from the locked cabinet.

Frank was glad for the morphine. It would calm him down and give them a chance to look at the wound. He sure wasn't going to like a finger digging in his arm.

Twenty minutes later a small pellet clanged against the metal dish. Frank was sweating bullets himself after he dug out the culprit. It had been deep in the stranger's flesh. He stitched up the wound and put a dressing on it, securing the shoulder with a sling. His heart rate was good. He would sleep for awhile. They had given him a pretty large dose when they saw how deep the bullet was in.

After washing up, Doc Roberts gave him a pat on the shoulder. "Go on home now, son. I'll take care of this patient tonight."

"Good working with you, sir. You taught me a few things I'd never have learned in medical school."

The old man nodded. "There are some things you find out with time and experimentation. It's your best friend some days." Frank followed his gaze when the front door burst open.

The sheriff came in, tipping his hat to Mabel and walked in the room to see how the stranger was. When he got a good look at the man's face, he whistled. A huge smile covered his face. "Why, I'll be a sonofagun!"

"You know him?"

"Sure do. Worked with this man many times over the years. He's a man I can vouch for any day of the week."

Frank got his jacket on, ready to leave while the sheriff and Doc Roberts talked. He wanted to get back to say good night to Mercy before she went to bed. It had been a long day. The crowd had thinned out now that the townsfolk heard the news the man was going to live. Frank walked down the street, his body weary from the events of the day.

He wanted to see Mercy and hold her in his arms. They were to be married tomorrow at the church and he couldn't wait. After tomorrow, there would be no need to say goodnight and leave her at the front door. The pastor had come to see him earlier in the day and let him know there would be a wedding right after the church service. Both Frank and Mercy had been relieved to know.

He knew Mercy was nervous about their upcoming marriage. Once the ceremony was over, he was hoping to replace her concerned look with one of wonder.

He didn't see all the commotion when he turned the corner at first. Lamps were on in most of the houses lining the street a block up from his house. It looked like a crowd of people were gathered in a circle.

Frank moved faster, searching the crowd for any sign of Deputy Wills, who was supposed to be patrolling the area. He explicitly heard David tell the deputy to guard the street like a soldier ready for battle.

Instead, Frank found Deputy Wills sitting up on the ground holding his hand against his head. He swayed back and forth moaning profusely.

He gave the deputy a hard look. "What's going on here?"

When Frank's loud voice demanded an answer, the deputy shook his head and stared at Frank. His eyes widened when he realized he was sitting on the ground. He tried to get up but fell to his knees. "I was hit on the head or something. From behind. I never saw it coming."

"Where is Mercy?"

"She's gone," a voice said a little further over. That's when Frank looked over to find old man Parson holding a smoking pistol in his hand. He knelt down to help the old man up and make sure he was not hurt.

"What do you mean she is gone?" Frank tensed. He looked at the mansion, which was right across the street and dark as midnight. "Did she go home?"

The old man shook his head. "I tried to help. Except when I fired the pistol the dang thing misfired and he knocked me down. I couldn't get up and save her."

"Who knocked you down?"

Frank already knew. He closed his eyes and sent a prayer to his Lord for the first time in months. He closed his eyes and held his breath.

"That lunatic who belongs in an asylum! He was hiding. I saw it all from my window. When I saw him waiting on Mercy and the deputy to pass by, I grabbed my gun and tried to get there, but I was too late." Parsons was starting to shake.

Frank turned to the small crowd watching. "Can any of you get Mr. Parson's to Mercy's house? He needs someone to attend to him. Martha is there and she'll take care of him."

"Are you going to find Mercy? They walked towards the creek." Parson pointed a crippled finger towards the west at a clump of tall pines.

"Yes. I will find her. Come on, Deputy Wills. We have work to do!" Frank was already heading towards the pine trees. He knew where the river was. There was a clearing through the trees where they'd gone swimming as kids. Since it was so close to the street and the mansion, Frank figured Thomas knew about it from exploring the area.

It was good he remembered the way. Frank stopped in his tracks when he saw Mercy lying on the bank, her eyes closed and her face pale. Rage rippled over his skin and embedded itself deep inside. He had to control it or she may get hurt.

"You can't just run in there and save her," Deputy Wills said, finally catching up. He knelt on one knee beside Frank. "We'll have to surround him and try to get her out of the way. One of us nabs the girl and the other gets the bad guy."

Frank stared at Deputy Wills. "I'll get the girl. You make sure you take him down this time."

Deputy Wills shook his head furiously. "I plan to. I have the element of surprise on him this time."

"I hope so." Frank didn't wait a moment longer. He swept past the deputy, crawled low on his haunches from one tree to the next until he was close to the river's edge. He watched the trees to make sure Deputy Wills was doing his job. He was. The man was sneaking through the trees like a warrior, which surprised Frank.

The moment the deputy stood and pointed a gun at Thomas, Frank made his move. He ran over to Mercy, picked her up and disappeared behind the first tree. He set her down, leaning in and placing a kiss on her lips. She was completely out. Her face was pale and she was motionless.

It worried Frank that she wasn't waking up. Her heart rate was steady, but slower than normal. Then he saw the small cloth tucked in the front of her neckline. Frank pulled out the cloth, the smell of ether causing him to hold his breath. He tossed it in the river, knowing the water would dilute it.

He tapped her cheek several times but she was out cold. Frank didn't have time to waste. He needed to wake her. The water wasn't warm enough to go in yet this time of year, but he had no choice.

As he lifted her up, he took a step in the river, it's calm current riding across his thighs. Frank walked further in until the water was waist high. He slowly set Mercy in the water and prayed she didn't wind up with a fever.

He looked up to the sky again, throwing out another prayer. *I don't call on you as often as I should. I need another favor, Lord. Save her. Please. I can't do it alone. Amen.*

That should do it, he thought. Inhaling deeply, Frank submerged her whole body and face with one quick movement. She needed a shock to wake her up. It worked. She began to spit water from her mouth.

"Mercy!"

"What happened? I'm so cold." She began to shiver and he knew he had to get her warm so she didn't wind up with a fever.

"Thank you, God!" he said aloud. He quickly carried her out of the water just as a horse and rider burst through the trees. That sheriff had great timing.

Sheriff Knight and two other men on horses following behind circled Deputy Will and his prisoner. The deputy had been holding a gun to the man's back, forcing him to place his arms around the tree. Frank wondered if the deputy had planned to take him in or stand there most of the night until the prisoner got too tired and fell asleep. The thought made him laugh in spite of the horror of the night.

Mercy moaned again, her lips starting to tremble. "I need to get her back."

"Give her to me," the sheriff ordered. He held out his arms while they placed her over his saddle. The sheriff ordered one of the men to give up his horse to the doctor.

Frank followed the sheriff out of the woods and down the street. The moment they got to Mercy's house, he slid from the horse and took her back in his arms. He got her inside and instructed Martha to gather all the warm blankets she could find.

While Frank waited, Martha stripped Mercy of her wet clothing and wrapped warm blankets around her, tucking them in.

Frank came back in the room, placing a chair beside the bed so he could keep an eye out for any signs of fever. He saw Martha had thought ahead to get a good warm fire going. He stirred the embers and threw in a few more pieces of wood. It wouldn't hurt to keep the room fairly warm for her sake.

She kept falling back to sleep. Frank was so angry that he paced back and forth, looking out the window. The men on horseback were taking Thomas Rider to jail. He had committed a crime and would be sent away.

Frank didn't care if he rotted in prison. Yet, he was a doctor and knew the man was demented. There was minimal help for him and he honestly didn't know if the man should be in a prison. There'd be no help for him there. He'd do his time and get out, possibly a danger to others. Or try to come back here. There was no way he'd allow that. He'd have to be evaluated by a doctor. Frank knew he had to do the right thing and get him help even if he wanted to let the man rot.

For right now, all he cared about was the woman lying in her bed, shivering under the warm blankets. He was prepared if she ran a fever. "Mercy, you get better. Our wedding day is tomorrow."

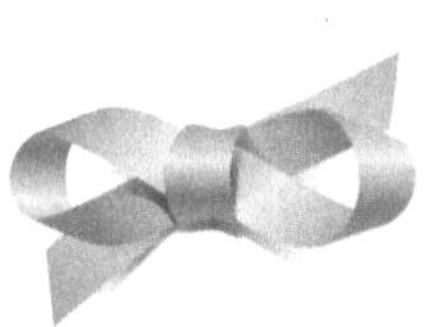

Chapter 10

The room was overly warm. Mercy didn't remember stirring the fire throughout the night. As a matter of fact, the last thing she remembered was that awful man holding a cloth over her mouth. She sat straight up and cried out.

The presence she felt by her side was not that horrible man. Looking into the eyes of the man she loved, she let out a sigh so loud, he smiled. "It's all going to be fine now, Mercy. I'm here."

She rested in his arms when he placed them around her. It felt so good. "What happened? All I remember -"

Frank placed two fingers over her mouth. "Hush, it's all over now. Thomas Rider will never bother you again. He's sitting in a jail cell."

"Thank God for that! He's a mean, horrible man. I tried to get away. Then he put ether over my mouth and it was too late. I knew what would happen and there was nothing I could do."

"Mr. Parson tried to save your life. He came to your rescue with his gun but it misfired and it knocked him to the ground. He told us Thomas must've knocked him down, but I examined him and there are no signs that happened. He's a good man to be so brave."

Tears fell from her eyes. "I must go see him before the wedding."

"He's here. They brought him here last night so I could keep an eye on him."

"Thank you. He means a lot to me. I'm so glad he wasn't hurt."

"Don't worry. It's all over." Frank took her face in the palm of his hands and kissed her mouth gently. "Do you know what today is?"

"I do."

"Are you feeling good enough to go through with our wedding today?"

She smiled. "I wouldn't miss it for the world. I have a surprise for you. I made a beautiful dress to walk down the aisle."

"I can't wait. Although, tradition says it's bad luck to see the bride the morning of the wedding, I call needing a doctor who happens to be your future husband an exception to the rule."

Mercy lifted her chin in defiance of the rules. "I heartily agree. I love you, Frank Mason. I can't wait to become your wife."

He stood up and bowed. "And I can't wait to be your husband."

He took her hand and kissed the skin, his eyes staring intently into her eyes.

Mercy wasn't nervous any more about becoming his wife. After what happened, she'd face everything head on.

<><><>

Frank stood alongside the paster, patiently waiting for his bride. The organ had been playing for a few minutes when he heard grumbling from the back of the church. "I'm not using a cane! I've got two perfectly fine feet! Let's get this show on the road."

The congregation turned heads to see what all the commotion was. Slowly, the bride and Mr. Parson began the walk up the aisle. Frank's smile grew so wide he was speechless.

She wore a beautiful lavender and white gown with soft ruffles and lace adorning the neckline. A sheer veil covered her beautiful hair and eyes. He loved her just the way she was but today, on their wedding day, his love reached new heights.

She was beautiful.

She was going to be his partner for the rest of their lives.

Frank forgot about everyone else, even the pastor.

When his love stood before him on the arm of Mr. Parson, he stared into her sweet face, unable to look away.

"Well, you going to stand there all day with that dumb look on your face or you going to marry the girl?"

The congregation gasped. A few trickles of laughter was heard since everyone knew old man Parson's demeanor.

"I'm going to marry the girl," Frank announced, holding out his arm.

"About time!" the old man mumbled, placing Mercy's hand in his.

He turned and wobbled a bit before taking a seat in the front pew.

"I love you," Frank told her in front of God and the whole church.

"I love you, too," Mercy said, a tear slipping down her cheek.

Frank took his thumb and wiped the tear away. They both turned towards the pastor, who had a bible open in his hand.

"We're ready now," Frank told him.

"Today, the two of you will be joined as one. Mercy, she is a gift to you, Frank, from God above. The same goes for you, Frank. You are a gift to her. Let me read a verse in the bible -"

He gazed at Mercy. She was trying to pay attention but couldn't stop looking at him either.

She leaned into him. He leaned into her. As the ceremony went on, as the pastor spoke his truth and the congregation listened, everything faded away as Frank thanked the man above for the gift of love he received. Mercy's gift. He'd treasure her forever.

. . ❧ . .

Thank you for reading Mercy's Gift. I've enjoyed writing this short story.

If you'd like to sign up for my mailing list, I'll give you a free book that will never be published. Go to www.cyndiraye.com[1] for more.

---

1. http://www.cyndiraye.com

Cyndi's Books

Mail Order Brides of Wichita Falls Series

Ruby

Grace

Lily

Charity

Hannah

Rebecca

Sophie

Ellie

Jenna

Leila

Boxed Set Vol 1-8

Christmas in Wichita Falls Holiday Book

Brides of Mill Ridge Series

An Outlaws Honor

A Reverend's Rose

The Ranger's Redemption

A Doctor's Devotion

A Teacher's Treasure

A Sister's Sanctuary

Sons of Nora White Series

A Bride for Luke

A Bride for Adam

A Bride for Samuel

A Groom for Nora

A Bride for Russell

A Bride for Wesley

A Groom for Widow Young

Multi-Author Series Contributions

A Bride for Abel - The Proxy Brides Book #4

A Tin Star for Christmas - The Belles of Wyoming

Candy Cane Christmas - Ornamental Matchmaker Book #10

A Bride for Calvin - The Proxy Brides Book #13

Mercy's Gift - The Belles of Wyoming Book #8

Contemporary Small Town Romance

Florida Keys Romance in Paradise Series

The Tomorrow Serial

The Forever Serial

Escape Serial

Island Keeper

No Name Inn Series

Boot Key Harbor Short Story Boxed Set

Santa's Wrong Turn & Save Me Santa Holiday Shorts

All these books can be found by visiting https://www.amazon.com/Cyndi-Raye/e/ B00ENA1WEG